LUCIDITY

Violet Rosenberg

Contents

Chapter One

She'd held onto hope that her life would one day find its way back to her, but that hope disappeared like kindle turning to ash in a fire. Her ex-fiancé was now planning his wedding to another and Hannah wanted to be happy for him. He was a good man and understood that her accident was something he hadn't signed up for. Lord knows he tried, but in the end it was easier for him to be her friend rather than playing the constant role of her caretaker.

But happiness wasn't something she'd felt for years. It was washed away that one terrible night and, Like Shawn and the rest of her life, hadn't found its way back. Hannah had come to terms with the fact that she was no longer the woman she was.

Once brilliant, always top of her class, she could no longer spell her own name. Always the go-to gal for a great speech, the words now tumbled out of her mouth, broken or disappearing before they could make their way out. She supposed it was easier now than it had been after the accident, when she couldn't speak at all. Strange how all the things she learned to do at a young age were now the things she struggled with the most.

Hannah's brain was still sharp, but no one would know it talking to her. Everything she was was now locked away in the confines of her mind, unable to find its way out. She could no longer express everything she thought or felt, not unless the other person had all the time in the world.

Despite her once vibrant personality, Hannah now felt like everyone's chore. So when her best friend from high school reconnected with her after finding out about her accident, it was almost like a breath of fresh air. Meggie didn't coddle her or treat her like a child. She never made her feel less.

The only time Hannah felt like her own person anymore was when Meggie called, and she needed more of that. Not just more of it, but less of all the other crap.

"You sure you want to do this?" Shawn asked, gesturing toward Hannah's SUV that was packed to the brim. "You have a support system here, Hannah."

Everyone thought she was crazy, especially her parents. But when Meggie told her about her roommate moving out then joked about Hannah moving in, something clicked. A new start. "I d-don't want a sup-p-port sys-st-em an-n-ymore. I just want t-t-t-o move on."

Shawn let out a long breath and looked like he was going to object one last time, one last ditch effort to keep her there beneath his watchful eye. But they both knew she was no longer his to watch and take care of. They'd both decided that and though he didn't say anything, she knew it was causing a strain on his relationship with his new fiancé.

And Hannah was tired of feeling like a strain to the ones she loved.

Shawn looked at her packed up vehicle, then back at her before running his fingers through his perfectly kept hair. Everything about him was always perfectly kept, perfectly organized. Perfect and now completely her opposite. "Call me when you get there so I know you arrived safely."

Hannah nodded and placed a small kiss against his cheek.

It was time to say goodbye. Like a breakup you can't move on from, her life had left three years ago and it was time to force herself to walk away as well. Time to let her parents enjoy early retirement without fretting over her. Time to allow Shawn to marry a woman who could take care of him as well as he took care of her. Time to stop feeling like a burden to her friends and family.

Time to make it on her own.

She'd already said goodbye to her parents, but Shawn felt different. Final. And despite the love they once shared and still shared in some small way, she needed that. Needed an end to their story once and for all. It was better for them both.

And as she got in her vehicle, giving him on final look, she knew he felt that too.

There was nothing to hold onto anymore in that town. Her final chapter had closed the moment the gun went off and she'd been living in purgatory ever since. Now, despite this being perhaps the most terrifying thing she'd ever done in her life, Hannah was ready to start her sequel.

Chapter Two

I t was a forty-seven hour drive from Maine to Oregon and took Hannah four days to complete. As soon as she arrived, she sent out a group message on her phone saying only three words, 'just got here'. If she used words any longer than that, the voice option on her phone would have struggled to understand her, replacing the words from her brain into random words in text. She'd had issues with that enough times in the past to only use single syllable words.

Once she arrived in Portland she changed the address on her GPS, a simple task for others but as she now struggled to spell, she read each letter one at a time from Meggie's text and entered it into the system, which took her roughly twenty minutes. Meggie would still be at work until two in the morning, working as a bartender at some dive bar not far from where she lived. Hannah was meant to go to the bar and grab Meggie's keys.

The GPS took her through a scary part of town, but never led her out of it. Instead, she arrived at her destination when all she wanted was to drive passed it as quickly as possible. Sirens blared passed her vehicle as she parked on a side street, forcing Hannah to cover her ears over her auburn hair. A delivery truck beeped as it backed into an alleyway next to the bar and passerby's yelled obscenities to a group of woman across the street.

This wasn't what she'd expected and wasn't something she prepared for. Her doctor's encouraged a calm environment and her symptoms got worse with chaos. Hannah couldn't help but wonder what the hell she was thinking. The chaos of this city, or at least this area of it, would set off the symptoms she rarely had to deal with.

After getting out of her vehicle and setting the alarm, she placed her hands back over her ears and hummed a relaxing tune in an attempt to drown out the noise. Tears pricked at her eyes as she struggled with each step across the busy street, horns honking at her and driver's screaming for her to watch where she was going. She stumbled before landing on the dirty, cold pavement, small rocks embedding into her palms.

She felt someone tugging at her body and looked up, seeing the face she hadn't seen in close to five years. Meggie's hair was now jet black, cut into a short bob. But her face still felt familiar and safe.

"Loud," was the only word she could force out. Hannah shook her head and wiped the tears from her face before placing her hands back over her ears. "Too loud."

"Dammit, David! I need a little help over here!"

It only took a few moments before a man showed up at Meggie's side. His fingertips brushed the hair from her face as Hannah continued holding her palms against her ears for dear life. "What the hell happened to her?"

Meggie shook her head. "I don't know. She said it was too loud, so I guess she's sensitive to sound."

The man scrunched down beside Hannah and glared up at Meggie. "So you had her move to Portland? What the fuck were you thinkin'?"

"I didn't know!"

Though he didn't appear very tall, he was strong enough to pick up Hannah's body with ease. She was tempted to fight it, but whenever Hannah felt heavily stressed, she became dizzy. Also, her motor skills were unpredictable, so maybe being carried was for the best. It was embarrassing, but so was running into something or having her leg give out on her. All Hannah knew was she had to sit down until her erratic pulse slowed and sitting down wasn't an option in the middle of the street.

"I got you," he said to her. His strong southern accent surprised her given the part of the country they were in. With each easy step he took, his shoulder length brown hair swept against her face and Hannah did her best to concentrate on the rhythm of that.

He looked down at her as they approached the bar. "Are you humming Simple Man?"

It probably seemed strange, especially since Hannah hadn't realized she was still humming, but that song always seemed to relax her. She wasn't sure if it was the melody or the lyrics, but she connected with it. "It c-c-calms me."

"It's a damn good song. One of my favorites." Then he smiled. Although he appeared genuine, the smile itself almost looked sinister, making the scar above his lip more prominent. The man, who Hannah could only assume was Meggie's 'terrifying' boss, had several visible scars on his face, neck and arm, making her wonder just how many scars he had that she couldn't see. Either way, she sensed he had a history as dark as her own.

Meggie held the front door open for them, but the bar wasn't much quieter than the outside. All Hannah could do was shake her head.

"I'm takin' her upstairs. You get your ass back to work."

"Since when do you go for the unconscious ones?" Someone out of view asked.

"Fuck off, Donny!"

Hannah closed her eyes once she felt an incline, his formally steady movements now becoming jagged as he carried her up the steps. He fumbled a bit to open the door once they reached the top, but as soon as it closed behind them, she was met with a blissful quiet.

"Better?"

She nodded before feeling her body set down against a soft surface. As Hannah removed her palms from her ears and opened her eyes, she was met with the sight of a spotless and somewhat bare apartment. "Do you—live h-h-here?"

"I crash here sometimes. Every now and then let one of my regulars sleep off the booze. That's why there ain't much to it. If you ain't got nothin, they can't steal nothin'. You want some tea? Helps calm the nerves."

All his words seemed to roll together as they entered her brain and she assumed he noticed the blank look on her face. "Tea?" he repeated.

"Yes, please." She watched the man fill a kettle with water.

He was muscular, which seemed more prominent in his shorter frame. A tattoo peeked out beneath the sleeve of his navy blue t-shirt.

"Somethin' tells me you, little lady, have a story."

She was certain by his tone that he was trying to be nice and make conversation, especially considering her having a story must have been obvious considering she'd just had a breakdown in the middle of the street.

"I'd give you the short ver-r-rsion, but even m-my short stor-r-ries take a while."

He chuckled beneath his breath. "I got some time."

"Meg-g-gie didn't tell y-you?"

He turned the gas burner on and turned around to face her. "She told me her best friend from high school was coming to live with her and she had some brain damage. When I asked how, she told me the rest of the story wasn't hers to tell. Meggie's definitely a firecracker. Only one of my employees that talks back to me, and she never passes on the opportunity. Not a month goes by where I don't fire her ass, but she keeps showing anyhow."

If she told him her story, Hannah knew what would happen because it happened every time. His eyes would glisten with tears that may or may not fall. His jaw would clench and his gaze would drop to the floor, unable to look her in the eye. He'd become quiet and regret asking. Things would become awkward.

But after everything he'd just done for her, it was only right for him to hear it. Besides that, he was a stranger who'd already physically removed her from the middle of the street and carried her up to his apartment, so things were already awkward. "There was a rob-b-b-ery at a gas st-st-station. I was—shot in the head."

His reaction was similar to the ones she'd received in the past, but his eyes hadn't glistened, unsurprising from a man like him, and his gaze never left hers. "That's a fucked up story. Lot shorter than you led on, though."

For reasons unknown to Hannah, she smiled at that. Since the accident, her loved ones began to treat her as a child. Since she could barely spell or read and had to relearn how to talk and walk properly, she supposed she must have seemed like one. But him treating her as adult was like a breath of fresh air filling her lungs and all her senses.

"What?" he asked when he noticed her reaction.

Hannah shook her head, suddenly feeling a bit shy. "You don't t-treat me like a child."

"'Cause you ain't one." His expression was slack, like it was the most casual and matter-of-fact statement in the world.

It may have been a casual response to most, but to Hannah it meant absolutely everything. Her being treated with kid gloves and being seen as one had put a damper on every relationship in her life, though they all meant well.

The kettle began to whistle and he raised it from the burner it was on to another one before going through his cupboards until he found a box of tea.

"She said your name was Da-David?"

He gave a quick nod and grabbed a coffee mug out of the drying rack. "And you're Hannah."

He placed the bag of tea in the mug and filled it with water before walking it over to her.

Hannah relished in the warmth it brought to her hands when she accepted it, or perhaps it was the warmth she felt within him, so very different than the man who'd spoken to Meggie only minutes earlier. "It's nice t-to meet you, David."

That sinister, sincere smile crept back onto his face, once again drawing her attention to the scar. "It's nice to meet you too, Hannah."

Chapter Three

Although Hannah was still awake, David closed the door as quietly as possible behind him before heading down the steps and back to the bar.

A girl that that didn't belong in this type of neighborhood. Any other part of town she'd blend in and probably adapt just fine, but this area was about as rough as Portland got and there was no way in hell she'd be blending in. People around here were the lowest in the city and he didn't want her history to repeat itself.

At least Meggie held her own. She might of been sex on two legs, but she put every man in his place; either under her heel, in her bed or out in the streets. Sometimes a combination. No one fucked with her and in the off chance they did, she made damn sure they regretted it.

When she came to work for him not long after he opened the doors, she'd been tempting and let him know that if he made a move, she wouldn't be turning him down. But David didn't fool around with employees and didn't get mixed up with her kind of crazy, as tempting as it once was.

While he heard she was phenomenal in the sack, not finding that out for himself was probably the best decision he ever made.

Meggie fit right in which was probably why she got on his damn nerves all the fucking time. How her and Hannah ever ended up being friends was beyond him and a straight up mind blow. They were polar opposites.

"What's going on?" Meggie asked when David approached the bar and sat on one of the stools rather than getting back to work.

He wasn't really needed anyhow. He had a cook there and there weren't enough people to help Meggie bartend, not that she wanted his help. They couldn't share the same small space for more than a couple of minutes before biting each other's heads off.

"Left her upstairs to rest."

Meggie sat a tumbler glass in front of him and poured him a bourbon. "You guys talk? You were up there a while?"

David glanced up at the clock above the bar and saw he'd been up there for nearly an hour, about twice the amount of time he thought. "Woulda been weird if we hadn't."

That comment earned him one of Meggie's signature glares, the kind you felt the heat of hell from. "Jesus, just tell me what you talked about and stop being a dick."

"She don't belong here, Meggie. Seriously, I don't know how the hell you talked her into coming here, but she needs to turn around and go back to where she came from."

"You don't like her?" Meggie asked as she set the bottle down and leaned against the bar, given him an eye full of the cleavage that earned her the best tips in a six block radius.

"I like her plenty." Too much, he thought; a thought he'd be keeping to his damn self. "A hell of a lot more than I like you. But craziness overwhelms her and there's enough crazy around her to fill a damn football stadium. When she gets overwhelmed, she gets dizzy and has mood swings and her symptoms get worse. I don't doubt that starting over was the right choice for her, but this is the wrong fucking place."

"Well, what is the right fucking place?"

David thought for a moment. He'd gotten to know Hannah a fair amount in the hour he'd been up there, but he'd still only known her for that one hour.

"Somewhere quiet with nice scenery, maybe by a small town but close enough to a city where she can enjoy it without havin' to live in it. A place that doesn't give her a damn nervous breakdown as soon as she steps foot out the front door. Where she can find a job that can work around her quirks."

Her quirks were very real symptoms, but those symptoms didn't make him think any less of her. Hell, they probably made him think more of her thinking about everything she's overcome. He could tell how much effort it took her to speak without drawing too much attention to herself, but David liked the way she spoke; slow and with every word having a purpose.

When he thought back to the laundry list he'd just listed, David got an uneasy feeling in the pit of his stomach that he foolishly tried to get rid of by downing his entire drink. "Fuck me."

Meggie pushed herself upright and grabbed the bottle. "First off," she began as she poured him another drink. "You only get one offer from me and you blew that sky high. And second, you better tell me what the hell's goin' on in your head right now."

David turned the glass around and around between his fingers. It was stupid just to think it, but bat shit fucking crazy to say it out loud. Yet no matter how crazy it was, the words still came out of his mouth. "With me. The right place for her would be with me."

He'd felt the second wind of her signature glare before looked up and saw it for himself. "With you? One hour with her and you're already talking about her moving in with you?"

"You haven't seen her since high school and you were ready to have her move in with you," David fired back even though he knew they were two completely different situations, his being the most ridiculous. "And not into my home, just the guesthouse."

"A guest house? Who the hell has a guesthouse around here?"

This was a part about his life he didn't like talking about and had zero intention of getting into it with Meggie right now. He wanted people to see the guy he was raised as; the son of a man who trained horses and a woman who owned and ran a hardware store and substituted at an elementary school. He didn't want anyone digging into his past as a soldier or the fact that he'd inherited a small fortune, though he guessed the soldier in him came out in his attitude and his need to keep everything clean and organized.

If Hannah decided to stay by him, Meggie would find out about one of those things, or just assume that he earned that small fortune in illegal activities like most did in this neighborhood. This was assuming he'd make the offer to Hannah at all.

He didn't know her that well and she knew jack shit about him, minus what she'd learned from Meggie. It would be ideal for her though. No one would fuck with her if they saw her hanging around him at the bar and she'd be plenty safe from that shit where he lived. He'd be able to keep an eye on her, look after her. She'd have help close by if she needed but still be able to live independently. No, they didn't know each other, but how well would they have to if he was just going to be her landlord?

And he didn't need the money so, assuming she received disability checks, he'd be able to come up with a fair price for her so she wouldn't have to rush out to find a job.

It still wasn't an ideal situation for himself. He built a house on fifteen acres so he wouldn't have people around. David didn't like people poking around his business and after a night at the bar, all he wanted was to surround himself with some damn peace and quiet. That's why he soundproofed the shit out of the upstairs.

David picked up his drink and brought up to his lips, speaking into his glass before taking a swig. "I don't live around here. And it's not really a guesthouse, just a livin' space above the garage."

He didn't want to come off as too eager about this scenario since it sucked for him. But he also didn't want Hannah to go back home with her tail between her legs because Meggie was too stupid to ask more about her issues before extending the invitation. "Hell, maybe she'll be fine livin' with you, I don't know. Just throwin' an option out there if she aint."

As he finished his second drink, he watched through the bottom of it as Meggie nodded slowly at him, clearly a skeptic with his motives.

Chapter Four

Hannah woke up in a bare bedroom, the only lighting coming from somewhere in the distance. It took her a few moments to remember where she was, realizing she was still in David's apartment. It was pleasantly quiet considering the space was just above his bar, and the blackout curtains kept the lights of the bustling city at bay. She could easily pretend that she was back in her much smaller city, no chaos surrounding her.

The problem was that the fantasy could only be lived in for so long. Eventually she'd be hit with the loud and busy reality that belonged to the outside world; one which her mind and nerves couldn't seem to handle.

She felt like a fool for the scene which occurred outside David's bar, but that would only be the first of many. Hannah couldn't come up with a way of staying here. If Meggie only lived a few blocks away it just didn't seem feasible.

Even where she was from, Hannah took night shifts after the city slowed down and the crowds lessened. Though she wasn't certain, this city probably didn't have a slow mode and as she peered between the curtains, she saw the streets were still full and traffic was still heavy. Hannah glanced at the alarm clock on the bedside table and saw it was just after one in the morning. On a Tuesday.

Hannah got out of bed, noticing that the sheets smelled like him. Stale booze and french fries. Not the best smells in the world, yet her heart sank when she left the bedroom and the smell disappeared.

The man named David was the polar opposite of Shawn. Though she met him only for a short length of time, that much was glaringly obvious. While Shawn kept his hair short and tidy, David's flowed like a wild river. While Shawn was tall and fairly thin, David was at least a few inches shorter but had the muscles of a linebacker. Shawn's skin was fair and void of imperfection while David's had a slight tan, showing a lineage she was curious about, and appeared covered in small stories she wanted to hear.

Maybe it was because he didn't know her when her life changed forever, but he looked at her and only saw her. That was perhaps the greatest gift this small adventure had given her, even if the adventure could only be short lived.

She opened the front door and immediately noticed the music was a fair amount quieter compared to before. As she began her decent down the stairway, Hannah quickly noticed the crowd had thinned out, only a few people at the bar, one of them being David, with Meggie behind the bar.

"You're awake!"

"I am." Single syllables. Though David didn't appear bothered by her speech, she didn't want it to be noticeable. The more she struggled, the more people noticed. If she took her time speaking and stuck to small words, she almost sounded... normal.

Hannah risked only a small glance at David before seating herself next to him. The next part would be hard to admit, but there was no way around it. And despite having only one conversation with him and despite being excited with the idea of having Meggie back in her life, she'd have to let them both go. So she took her time speaking again, saying each word as if it were its own sentence. "I don't think I can stay here, Meg."

Rather than look at her, Meggie's gaze fell to David.

"Told you," he muttered before taking a long slow drink from his glass. David, it seemed, had predicted this outcome.

"I wish it c-could work, but I don't s-s-see how it can." As she felt the disappointment fill her body, so did her nerves, causing her speech to falter.

"There is one option."

"Oh, Christ," Meggie breathed out. "You were serious about that?"

Whatever they were talking about had been spoken of while she was sleeping. Even if the option made no sense or couldn't possibly work, it was nice that he cared enough to think of anything.

"The neighborhoods loud and it ain't safe. Not a week goes by without someone's house gettin' broken into. I don't want you livin' there. Shit, I don't even like her livin' there and no one pisses me off more than she does."

"So, where would I live?"

His lips pursed, creating small lines to form on either side of his mouth.

Something about his silence spoke volumes. "With you?"

David picked up his glass and tapped the edge against the worn wooden bar, his grayish blue eyes remaining fixed on hers. "You can stay upstairs or I have an apartment above my garage at my house. It's about as quiet as you can get, just outside the city. Small lake and the nearest neighbor is a mile away. Either way, you'd have your own space. You can work here at the bar in the back and I could take you to work and bring you home, or there's a small town a few miles from my house. You could apply for some jobs there if anyone's hirin'."

"This is so fucking ridiculous," Meggie chimed in.

And it was. There were no two ways about it. It was absolutely insane.

"Why?" He barely knew a damn thing about her. She could secretly be a serial killer for all he knew. Of course, it would be hard to be a serial killer if raised voices freaked her out. And she didn't do well around blood.

Hannah really would make a terrible serial killer.

"'Cause I think given time, you'd be happy here. Plus, somethin' tells me it'll be nice havin' you around." The smile he gave her this time was much smaller than the ones he'd graced her with before with no trace of devilish undertone.

There wasn't even time to blush. Before her body could naturally react to his kind words or thoughtful smile, Meggie threw a dirty bar rag at his head. "Are you seriously hitting on her?" She didn't wait for his response. "She's been here for six fucking hours and was asleep for five of them."

David raised his hands in protest. "I'm just bein' friendly, you crazy bitch!"

"You're being horny!" Meggie countered with tenacity. "If you stick your dick into my best friend, I swear I will end your fucking life."

Though they continued to banter, David arguing that he wasn't nearly as much of a 'man whore' as Meggie assumed, Hannah just felt the need to laugh at the whole thing. Maybe he was just being friendly or maybe he was innocently and unintentionally flirting. Hannah was never great at telling the difference, even back when her mind worked perfectly. It took her forever to figure out that Shawn was trying to be more than just a friend.

But no matter what David's intentions were with his comment, he still treated her like he would anyone else by making it.

Chapter Five

Hannah gave staying at Meggie's a go for all of two days, never bothering to unpack more than a box of clothes. He had to give her credit for giving it a shot, but by the end, Meggie admitted that Hannah was a hot mess living there and Hannah agreed. On the third night, Meggie brought Hannah to work with her and she stayed above the bar, but they both knew that wasn't the right place for her to live either.

She'd shouldn't live in a place where going outside would cause a breakdown.

On day four, David picked up Meggie at her place before going over to the bar to pick up Hannah. He denied Meggie's teasing up and down and every which way, but couldn't deny it to himself. In the rough neighborhood where he'd opened up shop, Hannah was a breath of fresh air. He hadn't been around someone like her in a damn long time. Maybe ever.

He was pretty damn sure it wasn't a crush, just something different. Even if it was a crush, a sweet girl like Hannah had no place in his world. Someone like her needed a relationship, something he could not give her and would not give anyone. He'd been capable of love at one point, but that was a long time ago. A lifetime. Even though he was incapable of love, he was fully capable of kindness, and that was something he would give to Hannah freely.

He didn't want her to hate him. Didn't want her to be indifferent toward him. David couldn't live with himself if he'd made her cry, which he'd done more than a few times in the past once someone got too close, along with a couple of times with his employees.

When they went to pick Hannah up, it was still early enough where the city was as close to quiet as it knew how to be. This part of it at least. Anyone who lived or hung out around here would be sleeping 'till noon.

David was so lost in thought that he did the entire forty minute drive robotically, not realizing they were there until he felt Hannah's auburn hair brush up against his face as she leaned over by him from the back seat. "That's n-not your place, is it?"

"Holy shit, David! You never told us you were rich. I wanna fucking raise!"

He didn't live in a mansion, but a large one story cedar house, shaped like three out of four sides of a wide rectangle, with large glass windows all the way around, encasing the house with natural light unless you drew the blackout curtains. Between the two sides was screened in pool with a glass ceiling.

He had no fucking clue why he'd designed a four bedroom, four bathroom house since he'd always intended on living in it alone and hated having company over.

"I ain't rich, but my grandpa on my daddy's side was." And David had always and un-apologetically been his favorite grand kid. Where as the rest of them wanted the best presents and the best vacations, David just wanted to go fishin' with him. Wanted to hear all the stories of his younger years and wanted a quiet night by the fire playing chess.

When he passed after grandma, he'd left most of his money to David and some to his dad while leaving the rest of them with enough money to pay off their mortgages. Just under five million and all David wanted to do with it was build a house, buy his dream car and purchase his nightmare of a bar. There was still plenty stashed away since he was simple guy. Always have a rainy day fund, his grandpa told him.

The four car garage, which housed a car, SUV, truck and a motor-cycle, would be plenty of room for Hannah. She hadn't yet said that she'd stay, only that she'd look at the space.

"And you start doin' your fucking job once in a while and maybe someday you'll get a raise."

"Fuck you, I'm awesome at my job."

"This place is be-beau..."

The world trailed off into nothingness and David caught her re-flection in the rear view mirror as it turned from joy to sadness. She couldn't say the word.

David parked his car in front of the house rather than beside the garage and Meggie immediately jumped out and ran toward it.

Rather than follow her in, David moved his stare from the rear view mirror toward the woman he was looking at in it. "Take your time and divide it up if you need to."

A glimmer of hope passed through her pale brown eyes. Maybe she was used to being around people who grew tired of her taking too long to say something. Maybe it was just easier for her emotionally to let go of the things she felt she couldn't succeed at.

"It's beau—ti—ful."

"Thank you," David replied, both for the compliment and for the effort. He left the vehicle and opened her door for her, taking her hand to help her out even through there was no sort of drop for her to need assistance with. "Wanna see the apartment or the house first?"

Hannah looked between the two buildings, her gaze filled with wonder and excitement. She hadn't promised anything about staying, but right then and there David knew she wasn't going anywhere. She was already looking around as if this were her home, which David wanted her to feel to an extent. He just wondered what that meant for his own life.

"The house."

"Alright then," he agreed with a nod of his head. They followed the brick path toward the house, where Meggie was already waiting for him to unlock the door. "There's a small town about six miles that way," he said, pointing toward the right where the road continued. "Small grocery store with a pharmacy, bakery, coffee shop, book store, that sort of thing. Population's around sixteen hundred. They got a pretty decent farmer's market every Sunday there. Do you like to cook?"

"I used to," Hannah admitted, glancing his way. "I can't foll-ow rec—ip—es that well an-nymore though. Do you?"

"One of my favorite things to do." It was a part of himself that David didn't normally share. He'd originally wanted to open up a restaurant when he moved here, but the odds of it succeeding were too big of a risk. One day he hoped to build up the reputation of the bar enough to sell for a decent profit, then maybe give it a go.

He'd rather open a smaller place, maybe somewhere between the two towns where it could feel more like a neighborhood joint with just enough extra traffic to keep the doors open. "Don't normally follow recipes. Just go with my gut and hope for the best."

Hannah slowed her steps to a stop only a few feet from the front door. A light breeze made her auburn hair dance and brush across her face and David thought for a second that his heart might have stopped.

This woman was either going to be the death of him or his salvation.

"And what if it does—n't turn out like y-you hoped?"

Rather than brush the hair out of her face, David crossed his arms to fight the temptation and shrugged. "Just because somethin' doesn't turn out the way you hoped doesn't mean it doesn't turn out the way it was meant to. When you put your whole heart into somethin' at least you got the journey."

Though her lips turned upwards into a smile, Hannah's brows furrowed. "What happ—pend to the g-guy I've been hear—ing ab-bout? You are-n't mean like Meg's made y-you sound."

"Are you guys about done eye fucking each other?" Meggie asked rhetorically as she stuck one of her legs out and began tapping her foot against the cement. "'Cause I want inside this house so I can hate him more than I already do."

David shook his head, hoping the heat he felt creeping onto his face wasn't causing a blush. At least with his darker complexion it wouldn't be noticeable. "You gotta be a hard-ass to make it in that neighborhood and a hard-ass to do what I used to do. Doesn't mean I don't know how to be a good guy too, I just don't go 'round advertising it."

Her smile warmed every inch of his body and soul. It was the smile art inspired, the smile love songs were created from. "Th-thank you for being a good guy."

"You're welcome." As if he could be anything short of that to her.

Chapter Six

David had moved in all the boxes from her car into the apartment by later on that afternoon, leaving her to unpack them as he began to make them dinner at his house.

It was more than enough space for her, larger than the apartment she'd just moved out of. And it was already more or less furnished. Apparently this is where he had house guests stay rather than in the actual house, despite there being more than enough room.

Hannah placed each box in the area where it would be unpacked and worked on the bedroom first since the kitchen already had everything she needed in it and the bathroom had the basics. Almost every box for the bedroom was unpacked within a couple of hours and Hannah decided to head to the main house for something to drink in the hopes she wasn't intruding on David's personal space.

As soon as he'd pulled onto the property, Hannah knew there was nowhere else she'd rather be. Though it was only a few miles out of the city, it felt like another world. Only a few houses shared the lake in the backyard and he had a large garden filled with homegrown fruits and vegetables. His windows were so large that she could see straight through the house from the front to the back patio. It felt a little modern for him, but the inside had the rustic, simple touch that reminded her so much of the man she'd met only a few days before.

After tapping lightly on the front door, she saw through the large window him gesture for her to come in. She closed the door behind her and took off her shoes, just in case. Everything about his house seemed perfectly in order and cleaned perfectly and although he hadn't asked either her or Meggie to take off their shoes before, she didn't want to do anything that would make his life messy.

"Please tell m-me if I'm be—ing a nuis—sance."

He flashed her a gentle smile as he cut vegetables like a pro in the kitchen, his shoulder length hair tied back away from his face. "I think that would be the last word I'd use to describe you."

Curiosity got the best of her and Hannah set herself on a stool across the island from him. "Prom—mise?" She looked into his eyes when he glanced up at the word, but there was no sign of forced politeness, a look Hannah had become an expert at spotting.

David set down the knife and placed his large palms against the granite countertop, a shorter strand of his hair falling against his gray-blue eyes. "If I thought for a second that I wouldn't enjoy havin' you here, I wouldn't have invited you. Simple as that. And now that we got that out of the way, what can I get ya?"

"Some—thing to drink?"

"Soda, water, juice, coffee, tea, milk- that one's probably expired."

She couldn't picture him much as a milk drinker. "I'd t-take a juice."

David gave her one short nod and turned around, opening a cup-board near the sink and grabbing a glass. "I'll take you grocery shop-ping tomorrow so you know where it is."

"You've tak-ken enough t-time off, David." She hated that he took today off for her and didn't want him taking off a second. "I c-can fig—ure out where it is."

"That wasn't a question," David told her as he filled her glass with orange juice from a pitcher. "That was me telling you that I'll take you grocery shopping tomorrow. Besides, somethin' tells me everyone's havin' a better time at work without me there."

Hannah took the glass from his grasp and took a small sip, noticing quickly it was fresh squeezed. "Would you mind if I used your p-pool sometimes?" She could absolutely swim in the lake if he said no, but a pool told her how deep she was and she wasn't a very strong swimmer. "I used to go to the Y.M.C.A where I lived. It helps with my mm-motor skills. My left leg didn't work v-very well after the acc—cid—ent."

She watched as David went into a drawer in his kitchen, shuffling things around until he pulled out a ring of keys. "This one's for the front door. This one's for the patio door that goes to the pool. This one's for the garage. All yours, baby."

David tossed the keys to her and she caught them with her left hand just as her phone began to ring in her pocket. Since she had trouble reading, everyone had their own ringtone and this one belonged to her mother's cell.

"That's my parents," she told him, then grabbed the phone from her pocket and walked to the other side of the open concept into the living room.

Hannah swiped right to accept the call and sat on David's chocolate brown suede couch. "Hey, m-mom."

"Hey, sweetheart. You're on speakerphone. Your dad and I wanted to give you a few days to settle in. Are you settled in yet?"

She glanced over her shoulder to look toward the garage. So far she'd unpacked four boxes and three trash bags full of clothing. In her defense, this should have been day four of unpacking. She hadn't expected Goldilocks Sydrome, having to try out two other places before finally finding one that fit, nor had she told her parents. "Not yet."

"Don't procrastinate, kiddo," her father told her. "You wait too long and a year will go by and you'll still have boxes stacked and not even know what's in them anymore."

"How are you liking Meggie's place so far? Is it a nice house? Good neighborhood?" her mom chimed in. "You know, I went to Portland when I was about your age. Such a lovely city. So many places to go and great restaurants."

Hannah looked straight in front of her, noticing David staring back at her intently. "I'm n-not st-aying and Meg's any-more, act—u—ally."

"Excuse me?" Her father's voice was so loud that she had to pull the phone from her ear. Even David, who was clear across the room, seemed to hear him. "Just where in the hell is my daughter living then?"

Seeing as the conversation seemed to have caught David's attention, Hannah went ahead and put it on speakerphone.

"You know what yelling does to her, Bill."

"Yeah, well sometimes children need a stern talking to."

Hannah eyes narrowed at the phone. "I'm t-twen-ty-five, dad. And it's in a much n-nicer neigh—bor—hood and I'll get t-to live by my—self."

"Honey," her mother said, "We know you want your independence and we respect that, but you don't have a support system there. What if you need something or something happens and you can't get to a phone?"

Hannah nearly always had her phone on her and kept it fully charged. She even kept a battery pack charger in her phone just in case. "So I've gone from a ch-child to an eld—er—ly woman?"

Her comment earned a deep, quiet chuckle from David.

"You know we don't mean to imply that, sweetheart," her mother told her calmly. "We're just worried is all. No matter how old you get, we'll always be your parents and we're always going to worry."

The road to hell was paved with good intentions, but Hannah kept that thought to herself. They heard she wanted her independence, but neither parent seemed to fully grasp how important that was to her now.

She'd gone from a child to a teen to a college student living with her fiancé to an apartment one block away from her parents house. Hannah never had true independence.

"It's a great guest house with a l-lake nearby and t-the land—lord has a p-pool I can use for my phys—ical ther—apy. It's out in the c-country and there's a re-really small town nearby wh-where I can look for a job."

"How in the hell did you find a place like that in a couple of days?" her father asked skeptically. "It'll cost a fortune. I know you get disability, but you also need money for gas and for food."

Dear God, her father was a stickler for the details. If it wasn't his idea, he'd nitpick every tiny thing about everything. He was a sweet, loving man but using the word 'exhausting' to describe him would be putting it mildly.

"He's only ch-charg—ing me four hun—dred a month."

"What else is he expecting you to do for him so you can live there? Because I was looking at Portland apartments and a one bedroom costs a minimum of seven hundred and fifty dollars."

Even for her father, that comment was a low blow and judging by the look on David's face, he took offense to it. He walked toward her, doing a gesture with his hands, signaling her to hand the phone over. Hannah's shake of the head seemed to mean nothing to him, because David grabbed the phone from out of her hand.

"You wanna run that comment by me one more time?"

"Who the hell is this?" Her father asked gruffly.

"I'm Meggie's boss and Hannah's new landlord."

Before Hannah could hear either of her parents reply, David took the phone off speaker and walked out over to the patio door to stand out there, closing the door behind him.

She watched carefully as he walked around the pool twice, running his finger through his shoulder length hair, before finally sitting down at patio table. It wasn't until he appeared calmer that she took in the rest of the area.

On one side of the long pool was an outdoor fireplace with a couch and a couple of rocking chairs on either side of it. On the far end of the pool by where the patio doors led to the outside was a long eight person dining table. Across from the fireplace was an outdoor kitchen.

Curious why such a solitary man would invite her to live on his property or have a house this large and extravagant.

Hannah went back to her juice in the kitchen, keeping her eyes on David. He stood and stepped away from the table, his devilish smile on his face. When he reached the patio door, he hung up the phone before opening it and stepping through.

"They wanna come for a visit next month," David told her as he set the cell phone down in front of her, next to her glass of juice. "Told 'em I'd run it by you first."

It didn't surprise her in the least, especially now that they knew she wouldn't be living where she intended to when moving here. Maybe Hannah would take them over to Meggie's house so they could compare her living arrangement options. "I guess that would be f-fine."

"Also somethin' 'bout a guy named Shawn having business in Seat-tle in a couple weeks and wanting to stop by for a visit."

Hannah's eyes moved from David over to her drink.

While they both let go of the relationship two and a half years ago, Shawn had never been able to really move on, away from her. Yes, he'd met a woman not long after their relationship ended and yes, he was now engaged and in the early stages of planning a wedding, but he'd never cut ties with Hannah during that time.

Her reason for moving wasn't strictly about independence or about her moving on from her old life, but giving Shawn the space he needed to move on and start his new life. Now here he was, less than a week in, already finding his way back into her life.

"Who's Shawn?"

The two worded question had a much larger answer and like all her stories, no matter how short she tried to make them, they all took more time than they should. "We were go-going to start plan—ning our wed—ding after college. Then it happened and our rel—at—ion—ship ended not l-long after."

"He broke up with you?"

Hannah didn't need to look up to see his judgement. It was evident in his voice.

What happened between the two of them hadn't been clear to her until long after the relationship ended. It wasn't that he'd simply broken up with her because her symptoms became too much to deal with, but because she had become too much to deal with. "I p-pushed him away. He was go—ing to join his dad's com—pan—y.

Client d-dinners and parties. He n-needed some—one who he could sh-share that life with.

"Now he's ge-getting mar—ried and looks like he's move on, but he n-never did. I thought m-mov—ing away would help, but I g-guess not."

David let out a long, slow breath before sitting next to her. "Then you call him up and tell him 'no.'"

Was it that simple? Hannah would always love him, but the passion she felt for him was gone. After the accident, the passion she felt for most things had disappeared, but her 'can't imagine her life without him' feeling never did return.

"Listen," David continued, "I get where he's comin' from. A girl like you would be damn hard to move on from. But if he's given his heart to someone else, he needs to let go of yours. And if he hasn't given his heart to her, he needs to end it, because people don't deserve scraps of someone they love."

Hannah's eyes shot up to his, who met her stare with warm eyes. She had no idea what she was more curious about; his first statement or his second. "A girl like me?" She said the words slowly, each as sort of their own sentence, so she wouldn't stutter.

He broke their eye contact, stood up and went back around the kitchen island, returning to the task of cooking dinner. "Just sayin' it don't take much effort or time to care 'bout you."

"Do you care a—bout me?"

David glanced up, but only for a moment before he continued cutting the vegetables. "I wouldn't have offered up the apartment if I didn't."

It was an offer he'd made on the first night of knowing her after speaking to her for only an hour; an offer she was still confused over given the countless times she'd heard Meggie complain about him and share horror stories about what an asshole of a boss he was.

Yet no matter how much he confused her, David was right. Shawn's fiancé deserved his whole heart and Shawn needed to understand that the distance she created between them was not just a physical one, but a metaphor that it was time for both to move on and begin their new lives.

Chapter Seven

After a week, Hannah was completely settled in and, despite her protests, David and her had developed a routine. He'd get home every night at six or so, then make them dinner while Hannah swam in the pool. After they ate dinner together, they'd watch an episode or two of something and then she'd go back to her apartment while he went back to work. She'd awake to his headlight at around two or three in the morning. While she could have closed the curtains, Hannah liked knowing he'd gotten home safe and sound after sharing the road with all the drunk driver's.

She noticed the man worked on very little sleep and was surprisingly no worse for wear because of it. He'd still be up at eight in the morning, then invite her over for breakfast and they'd make small talk before he would head back to the bar at ten in the morning to open up by eleven.

"Any luck on the job front?" David asked while preparing dinner.

She'd told him that morning that she was going to head over to Ithaca, the small town he lived near, and look for a job. "No one seems to be hi—ring."

That was mostly true. The full truth was that no one was hiring a woman who had memory issues, couldn't carry heavy objects, had a stutter and a left leg that didn't always want to work, had anxiety attacks, a reading level of a third grader and couldn't write.

Honestly, she wouldn't hire her either.

"You can always come work for me."

"And what would I do?" She spoke slowly. It had become much easier to speak around him over the last week. David didn't seem to mind how she spoke, which put her at ease and made her more comfortable. She'd took her time saying each word as if it were its own sentence. While it took three times longer to say anything, she was able to speak with limited stuttering.

David had learned quite a bit about all her difficulties during their talks that week and knew what her limitations were. "I can take you back with me after dinner every night. You can clean off tables, do the dishes, clean up the kitchen after we close for dinner, then you can just hang out upstairs until bar close and get the place cleaned up and ready to go for the next morning. You can even wear headphones while you work."

Since it was the only offer Hannah had, it was tempting. With her low rent, disability covered all of her expenses, but she knew she'd eventually start to go mad if she remained cooped up in her apartment and David's house for much longer.

"I don't want to put you out more than I al—read—y have."

David glanced up at her, his hair falling in front of his eyes. "Do I look put out to you?"

"I mean, sort of." She was in his house at least twice a day every day and he did cook her two meals a day.

"Do you think I feel put out?" He rephrased.

Hannah shook her head. "No." The truth was that no matter how often she invaded his personal space, David seemed to welcome it.

"Think about it, okay?"

"Okay."

He went back to preparing them dinner. "Your mom called me earlier today," he said like it was the most natural thing in the world.

"And how did my mom get your num—ber?"

"I gave it to her. She wanted to know if they can come up for Thanksgiving and do a Thanksgiving and Christmas mashup. I told her I'd run it by you."

Christmas was her mom's favorite holiday. She loved to decorate the house up and go shopping for presents and look for the perfect tree. It always had to be the most extravagant tree on the lot, the kind that Hannah wouldn't be able to fit in her apartment. "Will Christmas trees be available by then."

"I can always get a permit to cut down a tree," David suggested. "There's plenty of space to put one up here."

Here, as in his house and not in her apartment. "David."

"I don't mind," he responded quickly. "Look at this place. It doesn't even look like anyone lives here most of the time. I'll buy the stuff and you can make it look like a home."

The way her said that caused Hannah to feel a bit flustered and she reminded herself not to read into a comment like that. "Can I decorate the bar too?"

"Only if you're an employee there," he replied simply. "So, what should I tell your mom?"

"Dep—ends. Is she cooking or are you?"

David glanced up again. "No one uses my kitchen 'cept me."

Hannah laughed at his serious tone, but his answer was the right one. She loved her mom to the moon and back, but couldn't remember a single Thanksgiving dinner that turned out properly. Something always got messed up.

"Tell her 'yes', so long as you don't mind."

He glared at her last comment, obviously growing sick of her feeling like a burden to him. "I'll call her tomorrow."

"And yes to work—ing in the bar, so long as I can dec—or—ate for Christmas."

His glare disappeared and the devilish smile took its place. "You start on Friday."

Hannah didn't mind the idea of working in the bar. She enjoyed being around David, knew he'd be a patient boss and liked the idea of seeing Meggie more often. Plus, she knew from Meggie that he had a firm 'no dating in the workplace' rule, which would hopefully keep her mild feelings for David in check and prevent her from making a complete ass out of herself, not that she stood a chance in hell anyhow.

Chapter Eight

D avid had a reputation in that neighborhood and in his bar. Stay on his good side and there wouldn't be any problems. Cross him and you'd wish you hadn't. It was simple and it worked damn well for him.

Yet on Hannah's first night, it became apparent to everyone around him that he wasn't as tough on the inside as he appeared. He needed his bastard reputation at work to keep his employees in line and to let customers know that fights wouldn't be happening. But when Hannah was there, things didn't work like that.

"You're doin' great, darlin'. Don't worry about it."

Whenever he said something sweet to her, Hannah would smile nervously and blush and damn if he didn't enjoy it every time. This last week had done a number on him and David still didn't know how he felt about that. He hadn't had someone so close to his life in years and thought he was making a big mistake when he offered. He liked his privacy. He liked to eat his meals in peace. He liked having no one around for miles. But one beautiful and slightly damaged woman had flipped all that upside down and changed his mind about his own life.

Hannah turned from the sink and leaned her body against the stainless steel countertops, showing him she was anywhere from damp to soaking wet from head to toe with stains all over her clothing.

"Oh yeah? You rea—lly think so, huh?" She looked down at her body before noticing food dangling from a loose strand of her hair and picked it out, flicking it somewhere in the room.

It was true that he'd been a bit overindulgent with his reassurance. She'd broken a bus tub full of dishes when she decided to carry them rather than having one of the servers do it. She'd spilled soapy water all over the floor of the dining area. When a small fight broke out between a regular and a drunk new guy and David had to jump in to break it up, she almost had a nervous break down and he didn't know where his attention would be needed most.

Truth was she'd crashed and burned that night. That didn't make David want her here any less, however. Not only did Hannah need something to fill her time, but he enjoyed her spending her time where he could keep an eye on her. Whether to protect her from the real world or to just look at her, David wasn't sure.

"Can't do much with the pants, but I got some shirts upstairs we could make work." She still had a few hours in her shift before he could take her home and he didn't want her stuck in cold, wet clothing the whole time. "Come on."

Hannah let out a heavy breath and blew the loose strand away from her face, then followed him out, sliding and losing her balance on the wet floor. David caught her before she took a nose dive and held her firmly until they hit dry land.

"Where you two going?" Meggie asked from behind the bar.

Hannah turned to face her and Meggie burst into laughter.

"I swear, I'm laughing with you."

Though she cracked a smile, that was about it.

David led her up the stairs and grabbed a set of keys from the pocket of his jeans. He unlocked the door and pushed it open, going straight into the bedroom to see what the options were in the dresser. The Rolling Stones shirt would probably the closest fit. It was from his college days, before the military changed his body. He couldn't bring himself to toss it and just hoped some drunk crashing there for the night would run off with it. David only kept his reject clothes there.

After grabbing the shirt, David went back into the living room, tossed it to her, then turned around so she could change.

After a full solid minute of silence, followed by grunt and whimpers, David began to wonder what the hell was going on. "Everything okay?"

"Is there a way you could go down—stairs and grab Meg without turn—ing a—round?"

It was like clickbait and it caught him hook, line and sinker. David turned to see Hannah visibly stuck in her soaking wet shirt, head somewhere in the torso area of the garment and her sleeves about a third of the way off. She looked a bit like one of those inflatable tube promotion things and he didn't even try to hold back his laughter.

"I told you not to look," she scolded.

"Come on, it's like telling someone not to look down. You can't fucking help it."

"Well, since you can't help it, c-could you at least help me?"

David went over to her and did his best to wiggle the fabric from her body, noticing her black lace bra begin to ride up with the shirt. "If I don't fix your bra you're gunna end up showing me a lot more than intended."

"I did—n't in—tend on show—ing you any of t-this!"

He could feel her getting flustered and knew that her symptoms would get worse and end up causing a panic attack unless he got her calmed down. "Deep breath, honey." He waited until he heard her take one somewhere inside the shirt. "I can fix the bra problem, but that means I'm gunna end up touching..." David began to fumble a bit at the wording, not knowing why he was having a hard time saying something he'd said a thousand times before.

"My breasts?" Hannah guessed.

"Yeah. Either that or I keep working at your shirt and do the gentleman thing and keep my eyes closed while doin' it. The thing about that is that I'm a guy more than I am a gentleman, so me honoring that could go either way."

"Just t-touch my b-breasts," Hannah muttered from inside her shirt. "You know what I m-mean."

David knew what she meant, but still got a hearty laugh out of it as he worked the fabric back down the slope of her breasts, trying to ignore how her pale, smooth skin felt beneath his fingers. "This bra is sexy as hell, by the way."

"Thank you?"

"You're welcome." When her bra was fixed, David finished getting the shirt off her body.

Once she was free, Hannah's arms immediately wrapped around her body, covering it up as if he hadn't already seen it.

"You don't need to protect yourself from me, Hannah. I ain't gunna cop a feel or nothin'."

Hannah looked up at him with her big doe eyes. "I th-thought you said you were a m-man be—fore you were a gen—tle—man."

"When it comes to sneakin' a peek, sure. But I got rules I follow here and the big one is don't start nothin' with an employee. That means I ain't gunna touch you, no matter how fucking sexy you look right now."

He watched as Hannah licked her lips nervously.

David was always honest, even if the truth sucked to hear and even if it got him in a little trouble. Something told him that after her accident, Hannah's self-confidence plummeted and for some reason, he felt the need to tell her that all the quirks and difficulties that came with what happened to her didn't make her any less attractive. Not to him, anyhow.

But as he said, he had rules when it came to his relationships with employees and seeing as he was also this particular employees landlord, if he ever decided to show her just how perfect she was to him, despite all her imperfections, it would be a recipe for disaster. Plus, they were friends and she was damn short on those around here.

So David held out his tee shirt for her and after a few beats, Hannah took it from his hand and slipped it over her head and David tied a knot in the fabric in the the front so it wouldn't appear as large.

He had a hard time figuring out which was hotter, Hannah in his shirt or Hannah in just a bra. The shirt came in a close second.

"Why don't you head downstairs and get the dining area cleaned up. No trying to move the bus tubs, though." Nothing she'd fucked up so far that night was a deal breaker, but he could only handle so many broken dishes before he'd have to place an order for new ones.

Having her in the dining area meant he could keep a better eye on her, help when it was obvious she needed it, and see how well she did in the atmosphere. David hoped to get her to the point where she could spend more than a few minutes in that part of the building without her ear buds in.

Mostly, he just wanted her to feel like she was earning her keep. A gal like Hannah, especially with what she'd gone through, didn't want to feel like she was being given handouts. She wanted to feel like she was putting in the work to earn her paychecks. He had plenty for her to do, David just had to find out what was a good fit for her and what wouldn't work.

There was a fair chance the dish room wouldn't work, but he'd give it time. He only hoped that everything else, like what he was feeling for the woman, would work itself out in time as well. Otherwise he'd be in a whole mess of trouble.

Chapter Nine

After a week of working in the bar, Hannah managed to get a handle on things. David weeded out the tasks that weren't working and replaced them with new ones. She eventually got used to the dining area, wearing her headphones to remain in her own little world. Hannah would fill the bus tubs, a server would take it into the kitchen, and she'd wipe the table down at sweep beneath it. As the dinner rush slowed, she'd sit in the corner table and roll silverware.

Once the kitchen closed, she'd wipe down all the surfaces and mop the floor, then clean out the dining section again. There was an in between time where, if the bar was slow, Hannah would hang out with Meggie or David would teach her something new. If it was busy, she'd go upstairs and nap or watch a movie until close. Then she'd go downstairs and clean up the bar, sweep and mop, then head home with David.

It all became less overwhelming as time went on. While it wasn't work she particularly enjoyed, Hannah was well aware that her options were limited and did feel like once she got a handle on her tasks, she was being of some use to David and making others jobs easier.

One thing Hannah did notice about her time there was the Meggie wasn't entirely exaggerating about David at the bar. He seemed like the opposite man she'd come to know while he was there. He was moody and ran a tight ship. Though his attitude toward her hadn't changed, she could see why Meggie had called him a prick all this time. Him being a hard-ass was putting it mildly.

He didn't put up with crap from drunk patrons, never gave out a free drink, wouldn't allow employees to waste downtime and generally always to appear on edge. Though David had the attitude and look of a bar owner in a sketchy part of town, Hannah wondered if he was this way because he was in the wrong business.

David had brought up opening a restaurant someday, which is where his true skills would probably flourish. But if he remained in this business for much longer, Hannah didn't doubt it would beat his remaining spirit down and his dreams would never become a reality.

"So, your parents are due on Tuesday, right?" Meggie asked from behind the bar.

Hannah nodded. "Dav—id and I are pick—ing up dec—or—a—tions and food to—mor—row, then he's going to h-help me put up the big stuff on Sun—day, and I'll stay home on Mon—day to fin—ish up."

"I haven't seen your parents in forever, but something tells me they won't like you working in a place like this." Meggie ran her fingers through her hair, exposing the neck tattoo of a series of colorful stars.

Meggie had always been a bit of a rebel, but her rebellious attitude appeared to have kicked in high gear when she moved away after high school. Like David, Meggie had a beautiful heart that she showed to few, hiding it behind a tough as nails exterior.

Hannah looked around the building. It wasn't as bad inside as the neighborhood surrounding it, But Meggie wasn't wrong. Her parents would have a few choice words about where she was now employed and probably about David himself.

Her family were upper middle class. They weren't haughty about it, but they did occasionally get judgey and Hannah was aware this would likely be one of those occasions. Despite David living in a house that rivaled that of her parents, he was still rough around the edges. His hair was shoulder length, sometimes pulled back and other times in his face. He was scarred, probably more than she already knew about. He wore permanent tattooed sleeves. He had a mouth that would cause a sailer to blush when he working.

There were other things about David that would fit right in with her parents, though. Not just his incredible house, but his good nature and talent in the kitchen.

Hannah was so lost in thought that she didn't hear the front door open, but did hear the whistle come from Meggie's mouth as it went from a high to low pitch. "Boy, did he take a wrong turn."

She turned to see a man wearing an expensive suit, hair freshly cut and face freshly shaved. Not just any man, however. But the blonde haired, brown eyed man who'd stolen her heart her sophomore year of college.

"Shawn, what the hell are you d-doing here?"

"I told you I'd be in Seattle for business," he explained as if were an actual explanation of why he was standing in the bar she worked in. "Asked your parents where you worked and here I am."

Hannah shook her head. "You're act—ing like that's a half hour drive, Sean."

He shrugged the comment off. "Wasn't too bad. I stopped to see a couple of friends on the way. I was hoping I could crash with you tonight, then head back in the morning, if it isn't too much trouble."

Trouble putting him up? No. But the rest of it reeked of trouble. "Why not stay with those friends you s-stopped to see?"

"They don't have a spare room and just popped out a baby. I don't want to get in the way."

The kitchen doors flew open and David stopped when his eyes landed on Shawn. "If you're here sellin' bibles, we ain't buying."

"I'm here to see Hannah, actually."

David had already let his feelings known about Shawn coming to visit her and while it was her life to live, Hannah knew he was right. As long as it was only physical space between them, Shawn would never move on and always find ways to close that space. But she also knew that even though she discouraged him from coming to see her, she couldn't just show him the door. There was still a friendship there she didn't want to lose forever.

"I take it you're Shawn."

"That's me." Shawn's casual tone only seemed to rile David up, who shot him a heavy and frightening glare in return.

"Why don't you go sit down at one of the bo-booths," Hannah told Shawn. "I'll be there in a min—ute." She waited for him to make his move, then walked over to David in the hopes of diffusing the situation. "I didn't know he was com—ing. I told him not to."

"Guess he can't take a hint." David's eyes were still firmly on Shawn as he sat across the room.

Hannah moved his face with the palm of her hand and forced him to look at her. "He wants to spend the night."

David pressed his lips together tightly and blew out a heavy breath through his nose. "I can't tell you what to do here, Hannah. I ain't your daddy and you got every right to have a guest over, but this shit's got trouble written all over it."

"I know," Hannah confessed. While a part of her would always love Shawn, she stopped being in love with him years ago and thought when he proposed to his girlfriend it meant the same for him. But Shawn had never moved on completely and Hannah worried about giving him hope. "But it's get—ting late and I don't want him driv—ing back."

David shoved his hands in the pockets of his jeans and did a sideways glance toward Shawn. A few beats went by and Hannah couldn't tell if he was pouting or really did have nothing to say. But he didn't have to say anything more to know exactly how he felt about the situation. He'd already made it clear and his opinions matched her own.

"I know you don't like this, Dav—id. I don't eith—er. But he's been a part of my life for sev—en years. I c-can't just turn him away."

She could walk away from her relationship just fine because of the dark place she was in at the time. But she was no longer in that dark place and didn't want to hurt him anymore than she already had. "So w-would you mind if I slept at your place to—night?"

David unclenched his fists and he leaned against the wall beside the kitchen. "No, Hannah. I wouldn't mind that at all." He ran his fingers through his shoulder length brown hair and glanced once more toward Shawn before turning his attention back to Hannah. "Why don't you cut out early and drive with him to the house? I'll try to get out of here as soon as I can."

Hannah nodded and placed what she hoped was a comforting kiss against his cheek. "Thank you."

Chapter Ten

"He's protective of you," Shawn spoke from the driver's seat as he drove out of the city.

There was no use in denying or underplaying it. "Yes, he is." Mostly David was just a friend, but he'd kicked it up a notch since Hannah began working at the bar.

"I'm happy someone's looking out for you here."

Hannah turned to look at Shawn. This was why their relationship was doomed and this was why she had to get away. Everyone changed their role from whatever it had been to her caretaker. While David looked out for her, it wasn't in the way Shawn was used to doing.

Shawn hovered and David gave her space.

Shawn tried to take care of everything himself, always in a rush. David took things in stride and only helped her when she was clearly in need of it. If she failed, it was her failure and not because she'd been discouraged from ever trying.

"Are you mad at me, Hannah?"

"Take the next exit." Hannah looked away from him and out the window. "Does Lil—y know where you are?"

"I told her I might stop by and see how you're getting along."

"But she does—n't know you're g-go—ing to stay at my place to—night," Hannah guessed.

"No, she doesn't."

Hannah mindlessly nodded. "You should tell her. And tell her that I'll be slee—ping in the other house to—night."

"You're making a big deal out of nothing, Hannah."

This wouldn't have been a big deal to her if they were still together and Shawn had snuck off to see his ex, then crashed at her place with just the two of them without talking to her about it first. "I w-won't help you s-s-sab—ot-"

"Sabotage?"

"Your marriage." She hated when he finished a word for her to get it over and done with. It was a little thing, sure, but it had festered and remained this constant thing hovering over her.

"Say what you're really trying to say."

She looked over at him. "I think you're st-still in love with the per—son I was and think if you hold on long enough, I'm g-go—ing to be that per—son again. But I'm never go—ing to be her again, Shawn, and I'm nev—er going to be fixed."

Hannah ran her fingers through her hair, getting caught in a snarl. "Lily loves you and you are—n't let—ting your—self love her back. Not the way you need to if you want this to w-work with her."

"So, you want me to let you go? Is that it?" Their was an edge to his normally docile voice.

Hannah wasn't sure what he was looking for when he came here, but whatever it was, it wasn't there for him to find and no matter how defensive he got, she needed to show that to him. "I need you to be—cause I need you to be h-hap—py. I need to be hap—py."

"Are you happy with him?"

"Take the next right," she told him. "And Dav—id and I are—n't t-to—geth—er."

"You didn't answer the question," he pointed out as he took the next turn.

That was because it wasn't an easy answer to give. "He d-doesn't make me feel broken. He helps me with—out m-mak—ing me feel use—less. He talks to me and listens like I'm a nor—mal p-person. He does—n't try to force the per—son I was be—fore the ac—cid—ent because he did—n't know her and doesn't see the worst t-time of my life w-when he looks at me.

"Yes, I'm hap—py he's in my life. I'm hap—py I have someone around who did—n't know me before and does—n't look at me like I'm a freak or tries to ba—by me."

"I never tried to baby you," he fired back with that same edge in his voice.

"All of you d-d-did. That's why I left."

The remainder of the ride was quiet and she saw Shawn's surprise when they reached the house.

Hannah knew people must have constantly judged David, just as they judged her. It was true he was loud and rough around the edges at work with eyes that looked like it'd lived six lifetimes filled with darkness.

People didn't see the gentleness within him, mostly because he didn't allow them to see it. They didn't see his good nature or talents.

"Some house."

In the little over two weeks Hannah had been there, she still found herself occasionally in awe of it as well. "It is."

Shawn put the car in park and looked over at her. "This David guy, does he treat you right?"

It seemed like such a silly thing to ask since they weren't actually dating. She lived in his guest cottage. She ate the meals he cooked. She worked at his bar. They shared good conversation and watched the occasional movie together. "He treats me great," she answered finally. "I know he does—n't look it, but he's a sweet guy."

"Then I should probably go, shouldn't I?"

Hannah was relieved he'd come to that conclusion on his own. She didn't want to force him to leave; didn't have the heart to. But if he had any chance of making it down the aisle with Lily and making something last between them, he could no longer hold onto the past. "I think it would be for the best."

Shawn nodded, then looked up at her apartment. "Mind if I use the bathroom before I hit the road?"

It was nearing one in the morning when her phone began ringing beside her, filling the room with Meggie's ringtone.

"Hello?"

"Okay, I don't want you to freak out." Meggie's voice gave her the opposite feeling, however. It was rushed and panicked, which was completely unlike her. "Some guys showed up to rob the bar tonight."

It was as if history was repeating itself, but she wasn't there to experience it this time. "Everyone's okay, right?"

"Not the robber's. One's dead, one's in critical I guess and the other should be fine. David's at the police station right now. It'll probably be morning before he gets out of there. He wanted me to call you and tell you not to worry or wait up for him."

David's request, much like Meggie's, was impossible. She took slow, deep breaths in the hopes a panic attack wouldn't take over. She was about to ask why David was at the police station and why in the hell would they keep him for so long. But before the question could reach her lips, Hannah realized she already knew the answer. "Dav—id was the o-one who k-k-killed him, was—n't he?"

There was a long pause on the other end of the phone that told her everything she needed to know. "It all happened so damn fast. One second the guys are yelling at all of us to get on the ground and the next second there were four crazy loud gunshots. I was too scared to look up, but then David yelled at me to call the cops."

"But he's okay?" She needed Meggie to say it. She needed to hear it.

"His arm got grazed by a bullet, but I promise you he's fine. Paramedics patched him up. He was more worried about how you'd react to all this than anything. He's scared that you won't feel safe here anymore."

That should have been the first thing on Hannah's mind, but it wasn't. The only thing on Hannah's mind was that David had just been grazed by a bullet. Every other fear besides that could wait. "Will you call me if you hear anything else?"

"Of course I will. And you call me if you need anything. I don't think I'll be sleeping tonight."

Chapter Eleven

Despite Hannah's best efforts, she'd succumbed to sleep watching television in David's bed. There was no chance of her going back to her apartment after that call. The moment David arrived home, she needed to see for herself that he was okay. And since it was daylight by the time she heard the front door open and close, she wouldn't have seen his headlights if she'd gone to rest in her own bed.

When she awoke to the sounds of him shutting the door and the metal of his keys hitting the table, Hannah pushed herself out of the bed and walked down the hallway to find him sitting on his couch in complete silence, elbows propped against his knees and his chin resting against his clasped hands. There was gauze wrapped around the bicep of his left arm, but other than that, it seemed only his spirit was tainted from the events of the night before.

"Look at me, Dav—id."

His head tipped back and forth above his hands. "I can't."

"Why not?"

"Not ready to see how you look back at me," David muttered.

Strange how he'd just killed someone, yet his fear seemed to stem from how Hannah would react to it. Yes, he may have taken a life, but she could never see him as a killer. So Hannah walked over to him, her steps sluggish from the lack of sleep, and ran her fingers through his shoulder length chestnut hair. "I could never be scared of you."

"Wouldn't blame you if you were."

"Well, I'm not. Just wish you had—n't gone and played the hero. You could have been killed, Dav—id."

"They'd be ironic. Survive four tours in Iraq and end up gettin' taken down by a low life shitbag lookin' for some quick cash to pay off his dealer."

David's head drooped a bit as she continued running her fingers through his hair and it laid to rest against her stomach. "I thought the days of me taking someone's life were passed me."

Hannah wasn't aware he was military, though it didn't surprise her when she thought about it. It was the reason why his eyes had so much darkness behind them, why he looked like he'd lived so many lifetimes of pain. "Please look at me."

He let out a heavy breath that sunk through her shirt and heated her skin before he separated from her just enough to look up.

"What do you see?" she asked.

"Everything good in this world. The kind of good that shouldn't be around a guy like me."

"I'm where I want to be, so don't even try p-push—ing me away bec—ause it won't work."

David shook his head, then slid his arms around her legs. "I got no intention of pushing you away, honey. I should, but I'm too big a coward to go back to livin' my life without you in it. Just wish I was a good enough man to deserve a woman like you."

Those simple words sent her mind into a frenzy, as if all her thoughts had just been tossed into a blender.

As she felt David's lips press against the fabric of her shirt, that blender was turned on high. "You're the one who should be pushing me away, Hannah. I'm no good for you. The man I was before I went overseas would have been treated you right. He would have charmed your parents, held the door for you, taken you on fancy dates, been given the green light by your friends.

"I ain't that guy anymore, Hannah. Now I'm the guy that doesn't hesitate to pull the trigger. I'm the guy that swallows that shit whole and carries it around with me everywhere I go. You shouldn't be around that sort of shit and you should run like hell away from me."

Yet all she wanted was to do the opposite, to feel the tender touch of the rough man she'd somehow tamed by her mere presence in his life. And she felt every last one of those touches like they'd branded her skin in the best possible way. The way his fingertips glided against the back of her legs and the way his hot breath felt against her stomach.

He was so much better for her than he realized. He saw her; not her former self and not the person she was stuck being after the accident. Her. No one looked at her anymore and saw the woman who was trapped inside. No one but him. He was her sanctuary from herself. With him, she know longer felt trapped in the body of a broken woman. More than that, she wanted to be the one who helped release David from his broken mind.

Hannah dropped to her knees in front of him and looked David dead in the eye. They looked back at her unwavering without so much as a blink breaking their stare. Everything he'd been through... she could see it festering in the shades of blue, speckled with the truth of his pain.

Like his touch branded her skin, the moment her lips touched his, every detail became branded in her mind; every hesitant movement, every breath he took in through his nose and the way his fingers felt against the skin of her neck when he allowed himself to give in. This wasn't her first kiss by any means, but it was the first since her accident that hadn't left her feeling crippled and lost. Instead, it helped collide the woman she was now with the woman she was before. Hannah found herself in that kiss and no matter how short lived it was, everything in the moment ensured it wouldn't be the last.

When Hannah opened her eyes, his were already open, but unwilling to look at her. "I'm not go—ing to run from you, Dav—id. I don't know what kind of man you were be—fore, but the man you are now m-means ev—er—ything to me. I d-don't want to go back to liv—ing my life w-with—out you in it eith—er."

Hannah stood on wobbly legs and held out her hand. "Come and lay down with m-me."

It may have been passed dawn by this point, but Hannah couldn't have slept more than an hour and he hadn't slept at all. David waited a few seconds before taking her hand and pushing himself off the couch, then followed her to his bedroom.

David undressed in front of her, letting his clothing drop to the floor until he stood there in only his boxers. Then he went into his dresser and pulled out a shirt, walking up to her and holding it out. "You can wear this."

With the closed distanced, she saw the scars across his body; a hundred stories told in the jagged pink skin. Hannah reached out and touched the longest one on his chest and saw his eyes close at the contact. Where his eyes told of the darkness within him, his tainted skin held the secrets he wasn't yet willing to divulge to her.

He handed her the shirt in silence before crawling into the bed, proof he wasn't yet willing to talk to her about the scars. Hannah knew it would take time to get there, to hear all his past escape from his lips and feel safe in her knowing that truth. And she wouldn't push him for that truth just as he wouldn't push her to go into detail about her own. He knew of the accident, but not of all the pain that came with it.

Rather than go into the bathroom to change, Hannah turned to face the wall and undressed there before sliding the shirt over her head until it fell just above her knees. She didn't want to hide from him. Hannah felt like she'd been hiding from the world for the last three years. For the first time in what felt like thousand years, she wanted to seen; truly seen.

"You're so damn beautiful, Hannah. Bein' around you these last two weeks, I sometimes forget to breathe just lookin' at you or listenin' to you."

She turned to look at him laying on the bed with his scarred chest exposed and his hair splayed across his pillow. If any man was ever 'beautiful' to her, it was David. He didn't remind her of any man she'd known before him and most definitely wasn't the typical kind of beautiful. His skin had been sliced and punctured, his eyebrows were naturally raised almost as if he were forever calling 'bullshit' on something and his mouth gave the same impression with a slight curve seeming to always appear on one side as if there was always a secret he was taunting you to tempt out of him. And while she never used to find longer hair particularly attractive on a man, she'd been fighting temptation to run her fingers through it up until that night when she was finally able to do just that.

It wasn't just his looks that made him deceptively beautiful to her, but the way he saw beauty in her flaws.

"Tonight all I could think about was your face and wonderin' if there was some small detail I missed and wouldn't get a chance to see. You were the only thing on my mind, darlin'. Even when it was over, all I could think about was gettin' back home to you."

David, she could tell, was not the man who gave his heart to another freely. He was the kind of man who kept it under lock on key, refusing to let emotion take hold over the physical. She knew from Meggie that he was strictly a one night stand kind of guy, but that rule seemed far from strict the way he was looking at her now.

Still, looks could be deceptive and he had just gone through something that left him feeling vulnerable and Hannah didn't want to
mistake that for something else. He was her landlord as well as her
boss and if she mistook this whole thing, it could only lead them
toward disaster.

"Come lay down next to me and tell me what's on your mind,
'cause it don't look good."

Hannah did as he asked, well.. told, and went and laid next to him,
covering her body with the blanket. "I'm try—ing not to r-read into
this."

"Into what, darlin'?"

He pulled her body next to him and she rest her head against the
large scar on his chest. "All of t-this. I know you have r-ru-rules when
it comes to wo—men and when it comes to em—ploy—ees."

David let out a heavy breath through his nose and squeezed her
tighter. "There's an exception to damn near every rule, and you are
my exception, Hannah. I ain't never been much afraid of dyin' until
tonight, but I was afraid of never bein' able to see you again."

Chapter Twelve

A knock on the door woke them from a dead sleep and David looked at his phone and saw it was a little passed noon. Hannah stirred beside him, opening her sleepy dark eyes slowly. "Stay here, darlin'."

David placed a soft kiss against the tired woman in his bed, relishing in the soft moan she made at the small gesture, then grabbed his clothes from the night before and quickly dressed in the hallway.

It hadn't been his intention to ever start anything with Hannah. David had figured his growing infatuation with her would eventually subside and in time she'd be nothing more than a good friend.

Fate had other plans for him, he came to find out. When he looked at the gun, her face was the only one that passed through his mind, over and over again playing like a movie and showing him what his life could be if only he gave real living a chance. Last night was his wake up call and damn if he didn't enjoy waking up with her by his side.

It had been a long time since he'd allowed himself to feel anything more than physical with a woman in his life and David, as much as he tried, couldn't stop himself from feeling everything when it came to her.

He was sliding his shirt over his head when he entered the living room and saw Meggie standing on the other side of the door, her beat down piece of shit Buick parked behind her by the garage. David had expected the cops to be on the other side of the door since they mentioned something about stopping by to ask some more questions, but it wasn't too surprising that Meggie was here.

After opening the door for her, David stood to the side to let her pass. "Hey."

"I expected you to look more like shit," Meggie spoke in her usual dry, semi-snarky tone he'd come to hate and enjoy.

"Sorry to disappoint. Whatcha need?"

Meggie dropped her oversized purse by the door and her jacket next to it and David had to stop himself from cleaning up the mess. "I wanted to check in on Hannah, but she didn't answer the door. Also wanted to see what you planned on doing about the bar."

"She's still in bed," David explained.

Meggie's piercing pale green eyes narrowed on him. "Her bed?"

David stared at her for a good few seconds before running his fingers through his bed head. "We should keep the bar closed 'til Black Friday, give everyone a few days off for the holiday. I'll compensate everyone for lost wages, but I think they all need some time to cope with what went down and gives me some time to find a cleanup crew."

"Please tell me you didn't fuck my best friend with your disease ridden dick, David."

He glared back at her. "I didn't fuck your best friend and my dick is happy and healthy, thank you very much, and none of your goddamn concern."

Yes, David could be considered a man whore. He hadn't done commitment for a good fifteen years at least and Meggie had bared witness to the women he took up to the apartment above the bar. But he was also checked regularly and never had sex without a condom.

Meggie knew he was a dick and dash kind of guy and that Hannah was not a fuck 'em and leave 'em kind of girl. All this probably spelled disaster to her, but David wasn't just willing to try to be the man Hannah deserved, he wanted to be, which was a damn unnerving thought.

Meggie crossed her arms and glared at him right back. "If you fuck with her, I will wear the pointiest boots you've ever fucking seen in your life, pierce your balls with them and quit on the spot. Then I'll wait a month before I burn that shit hole of a bar to the ground with you locked inside of it. Do you get me?"

It was no secret that Meggie was a damn terrifying woman, which was one of the main reasons he hired her. She was actually a shitty bartender at first, but she was hot and she was tough, so he gave her time to work on the skill part of the job.

"Hey!" Hannah sang out, still braless in his shirt but wearing jeans. "What are you two talk—ing about?"

"Just warning me about breakin' your heart or screwin' with your head or somethin' like that," David told her, keeping his eyes on Meggie.

"Please, she'd break your jaw if you did."

"Death by fire, actually," David corrected.

Hannah walked to his side and looked at Meggie with scrunched up eyebrows. "That's a bit of an ov—er—kill, is—n't it?"

Meggie shrugged. "I don't think so. Did that hot ass ex of yours leave already or were you two going to spend the day together."

David was embarrassed to admit even if only to himself that he'd forgotten about the Bible salesman staying over, or the fact that he existed at all, but looked passed Meggie and didn't see an extra car anywhere.

"I sent him back to Se—at—tle as soon as he dropped me off. I th-think we both knew it w-was for the best."

He didn't doubt that one of them knew is was for the best, but something told David that she made it obvious she was less than thrilled with the idea and he decided not to stay where he wasn't wanted.

David felt for the guy. Though he hadn't been in the same spot as him, he'd been in a similar one where the first and only love of his life was in a dark place after her twin sister's death while he was serving overseas. She went downhill fast until the woman he fell in love with just wasn't there anymore. He hung in there for a good year and a half, but finally called it quits when he was being sent home on leave and realized he didn't look forward to seeing her.

Situations changed people. Sometimes they bounced back and found their way back to themselves, but everything a person goes through has at least a small impact on who they are.

But if the the Bible Salesman tried anything with Hannah again, David's fist would be making an impact on the guys face.

David wrapped his arm around Hannah and pulled her against him, placing a kiss on her forehead. "Thank you," he whispered against her skin. He kissed her again before letting her go. "You ladies want some breakfast or lunch or somethin'?"

Meggie tilted her head and stared at him. "I think we should talk about what happened last night. You know, when you killed someone."

His mind went back to when he'd first killed after they'd walked into an ambush. He remembered pulling the trigger on instinct when he saw the gun pointed at his truck twenty feet out. It was the most surreal feeling he'd ever had, but it was cut short by the fact that there were still men shooting at him and his friends. There wasn't even time to think about the biggest moment in his life while it was happening.

When everything subsided around them, it finally sunk in. He'd taken four lives in probably five minutes or less. All of them were someone's son, some father's and husband's. All had lived out their lives the only way how until he took those lives away.

Like probably everyone else did, he told himself he'd deal with those emotions when the time was right because in war, if you let that stuff get to you, it could cost you your life or the life of one of the men at your side.

Once he returned to civilian life, it had become a constant battle. He went to the meetings, went on medication to help him sleep, but the first year was hell. He'd opened a bar hoping to keep his mind busy, but it ended up being the sanctuary of this house that brought him the peace he needed.

That past would always be a part of him, however. Not a day went by where he didn't think about the lives he'd taken or hated himself for not knowing just how many times he'd killed. Whether killing on a battlefield or killing at the bar, it was all the same. David was still in charge of protecting his employees and it was still survival instinct. The only difference was that bar would no longer serve as a distraction, but as a reminder of what'd he'd done inside those four concrete walls.

"Break—fast sounds good," Hannah said by his side. "We should prob—ab—ly hur—ry, though. We still have to go groc—ery shop—ping and get dec—or—at—ions for the house to—day."

He loved her for that and the thought caused his entire body to tense.

"I'm not hungry," Meggie muttered across from the. "I'm confused and annoyed, but not hungry. We need to talk about this, David. Everyone is going to want to talk about this. It's not just something you can sweep under the rug."

Like hell he couldn't. David had done just that time and time again and knew eventually his life would be rearranged and the rug would be re-placed. But he wasn't going to open that wound until the holidays had passed, after Hannah's family had come and gone. Then, he'd go and find a meeting and talk to the people who wouldn't just empathize, but understand from personal experience.

David let Hannah go and went into his bedroom, removed the art print from the wall and turned the dial of his safe. He didn't bother counting the money, just grabbed a couple of stacks of hundred dollar bills and closed it all up.

Then he went into the kitchen, grabbed the list of the names and numbers of all his employees, then walked into the living into the living room and handed the stack to Meggie, along with the list. "Call everyone up and have them meet you somewhere. Give the kitchen crew a couple hundred bucks for lost wages, the bartenders and waitress three for lost tips and you can keep whatever's left. Tell them we'll open again on Friday and if anyone doesn't to return, I understand and to call me so I can cut 'em a paycheck for two weeks while they look for another job."

Meggie's eyes remained on the stack of money in her grasp for a good half minute before looking up at him, then at Hannah, then back at him. "You're paying me off so you don't have to talk about it."

"I can't talk about it," David corrected quietly. "I'm paying you extra as a bonus. I want to promote you to manager."

"Manager," Meggie repeated. "You're manager."

David shook his head. It wasn't something he'd thought about until he spoke the words, but his head would never be in the game at the bar. Not anymore. It would never be a place he'd enjoy being in from this day forward and if he was really going to try this thing with Hannah, his night of drunkenness and debauchery would have to come to an end.

Since she'd entered his life, all he wanted to do was get his shifts over with and get back home. Even if was asleep in her own apartment, she was still closer and that closeness had brought him a peace like nothing else.

After what happened last night, David knew two things.

The first, he no longer wanted to live a wasted life. He wanted to feel at least some small sense of pride in what he did day in and day out. He didn't want to keep pushing off any dreams he had, telling himself he had plenty of time left or that they were a fools dream.

The second, he wanted someone by his side when he made those dreams come true.

None of that would happen at the bar. It was just a place to fill his time so he wasn't just living his life on an inheritance.

He wanted to build furniture again, like he did when he'd just got out of the military. He wanted to open up the restaurant that had been his unspoken dream he was too afraid to chase for years.

"Not anymore," he finally told her. "If it ends up being something you really want, we'll figure out a land contract." David shook his head, ran his fingers through his hair, and let out a heavy breath. "I can't keep living that life, Meggie. It might look like a good fit for me, but I just changed who I was to fit where I was. I don't want it anymore. I wanna be the kind of guy that deserves the kind of girl standin' next to me."

Chapter Thirteen

David remained true to his word. Hannah felt like she was living in a Hallmark movie for two days. He readied his house for her parents visit, cutting down a tree, decorating with her as he played French Christmas music over the speakers in the living room. That was also how she learned he spoke French, then found out he also spoke Latin, Spanish, German and Italian. Not all of them fluently, but hearing him whisper Italian into her ear was enough to get her lady parts antsy.

When it came to sex, however, David wanted to wait for a while. It was crazy frustrating considering how dead sexy and sweet he'd been since the accident, but Hannah did her best to show restraint.

They decorated the house, bought the groceries and David redecorated the guest bedroom using furniture he'd made that was hiding away in a workshop she hadn't even known was on the property.

The man went from brooding bar owner to fully domesticated in the blink of an eye and Hannah couldn't help but wonder if the transformation would last or if it was simply a reaction to Saturday's turn of events that would fade over time.

"What time does your parents plane land?" he asked as he re-arranged all the odds and ends in the living room."

"4:30."

It was the third time he'd asked that day alone and Hannah was a bit amused at how antsy David was about meeting her parents. He hadn't exactly said they were dating yet and they'd only kissed a few times, but she guessed this was a bigger deal for him now than when they'd made the plans originally.

"What time is it now?"

David lifted the sleeve of his navy blue sweater and checked his watch. "Almost a quarter after three. We need to leave here in about half an hour." He took a break from his obsessive tidying up and walked over to her. "So, how are we going to do this? Are we just going to stick to what they already know, me being your landlord, or..."

Hannah raised an eyebrow and smiled when she noticed a slight blush on his dark skin. "Or?" She wasn't going to be the first to say it because she still didn't know what the hell they were.

"Or are we going to call me something else?" David put his arms around her waist.

"Like what? Like 'Dav—id'?" Hannah teased.

David let out a breath through his nose and narrowed his blue eyes at her. "Like your bo-... boss?"

Hannah didn't hold back her laughter. "You can't s-say it, can you?"

"I can say it," David pouted.

Hannah tilted her head up to look at him. "So are you? My bo-boss?"

That devilish smile appeared on his face. "Do you want me to be?"

"Depends. You think you can tame your wild ways and be a one wom—an kind of guy?" Hannah asked him.

It was a fair question to ask. While she hadn't seen any of it since she'd been here, she'd heard about his reputation. Even before deciding to move here, Meggie couldn't help but vent about her crazy, moody man-whore of a boss.

She knew everyone had a side they didn't show others easily, but she also wanted to know that if she went for something with him, Hannah wouldn't be left without a home and full of regret.

"I know I can, darlin'. I've just been waiting on a woman to make it worth my while. And you are more than worth my while."

Hannah looked down to hide her own blush. The southern man in front of her had a way with words that always seemed to leave her skin flushed, her head spinning and her legs a wobbly mess. "I guess you can t-tell them you're my boy—friend then."

"I just might do that," David agreed quietly above her. "So, do you think I'll gain their approval?"

"P-prob—ab—ly not. But in their def—ense, no one is good en—ough for me."

"Not even the Bible guy?"

Hannah laughed as she shook her head. "Not un—til af—ter the break—up."

They never hated him. They never gave him too hard a time and never tried to put an end to the relationship. Instead they'd been indifferent. Neither of her parents had tried to bond with him and weren't deliriously happy when she'd announced her engagement to Shawn.

After the accident, however, Shawn had truly stepped up and was there for her and her parents saw that. But he was there for her the way they were, not the way she needed him to be. He'd taken care of her in all ways, but the fire was gone and Hannah had given up waiting for its return.

Shawn would always love her, of that Hannah had no doubt, but the passion was gone. He was just holding on because moving on was too terrifying of a concept for him.

"We should get going," David told her, breaking Hannah from her thoughts. "Traffic is going to start picking up soon."

"Can't ev—en spare a min—ute?" Hannah asked, trying her best to sound flirtatious. She wrapped her arms around his torso, resting her hands against his lower back.

David flashed her a warm smile rather than his usual devious one. "Just one?" He lowered his nose to beneath hers and lifted her head that way. "For you I could probably manage to spare two."

He parted her lips with his own, kissing her with such perfection and gentleness that he felt like a soft breeze breathing life into her uncertain world. His kisses were new to her, but felt so familiar, as if the universe brought her to him. She supposed in a way it had. Fate had taken a hold of her life in so many ways, leading her to exactly where she was meant to be.

Her hands repositioned themselves to his hair, grasping the stands as she pulled him closer. How someone so rugged and tough could hold her and kiss her so much tenderness made her heart soften. This was the man he was for her and her alone, like a secret she wanted to share with the world, yet also wanted to keep all to herself.

When she felt his tongue skim the tip of her own, Hannah tried to deepen the kiss to no avail. He was a man in constant control of his world and she wanted desperately for him to lose that control; to kiss her without hesitancy. Without holding back.

"Hannah," he warned in a hire voice than normal.

She'd tried time and time again over the last few days for him to give her the hard, passion filled kiss she'd been so desperately craving. He'd been the first man she'd kissed since Shawn and even before then, he rarely kissed her unapologetically. As much as Hannah enjoyed sweet, she also enjoyed a little salt and had been without for too damn long.

David was nothing if not a passionate man and she knew if she could only get him to open up physically, he'd give her that roller coaster of desire and heat she was dire need of.

"You d-don't have to be so gen—tle with me, you know. I won't break."

"Maybe I'm worried I'll break," David replied quietly against her lips. "Maybe I'm takin' it easy on myself because I know once I dive in, I'm gonna drown in you, and that ain't somethin' I'm used to feelin'."

His words were like a fire creeping across the surface of her skin. For someone with poor grammar, he certainly had a way of talking that left her feeling dizzy and unable to form a coherent thought. "What if I want you to d-drown in me?"

"I fully intend to," David answered, his voice barely above a whisper before he took I step back. "After your parents have come and gone, so I don't have to be forced to think about what I'm missin' out on while they're here. And speaking of your parents, your two minutes are up and it's time to go pick 'em up."

Chapter Fourteen

As soon as David put his shiny black SUV in park, the horn of the vehicle behind them was blaring in her ears. Hannah had given up listening to her music about twenty minutes ago with nothing being able to drown out the sound of the anxious park and goers. David had timed it fairly perfectly, having done this numerous times for his own family over the last few years.

He'd had Hannah keep an eye on the flight online for any delay or early arrival, seeming to know roughly how long it would take them to pick up their bags and navigate their way to the front doors of the airport. Apparently he didn't want to be one of 'those drivers', who'd gotten there half an hour early and held up the line.

Hannah opened the sunroof of the SUV and popped her head up, scanning the crowds of any sign of her parents. When she caught sight of her mom's 'travel-wear', the signature gaudy Panama hat with an electric yellow ribbon she wore so she could easily be spotted in a crowd if anyone ever got separated, Hannah waved her hands about until her mother spotted the gesture. "Found them!"

David popped the hatchback of the SUV, telling her to stay inside since he knew this sort of hectic atmosphere could cause an anxiety attack in five seconds flat. So she watched from the passengers seat as David gave her dad a firm handshake, ignoring as he stared at his longer hair. Her mother gave him a gentle hug and afterwards he grabbed the bags from her hands and walked them to the back of the SUV.

She heard her dad comment at the vehicle's gas mileage.

"I don't use it that often. I try to drive it at least once a month so things don't start goin' to hell on it, but usually just into town to go grocery shopping."

Her dad was a nit picky man, and that was putting it mildly. She loved him to the moon and back, but he was a difficult guy to impress. He always found some hidden flaw or some minuscule negative to focus on, which didn't take long to become agitating.

This was the first time in three weeks she'd been in this vehicle and David's fuel economy was hardly any concern to her dad.

But Shawn had gone through something similar, as did the boys she dated in high school, so Hannah chalked it up to an initiation of sorts. If David could make it to the end of the weekend without punching her father in the face, the visit would be considered a success.

She watched as David opened the back door for her mother, then closed it behind her before trotting to the other side of the car to take his place behind the wheel.

"Looks like you found yourself a real southern gentleman there," her mother sang out from the backseat.

"They aren't dating, remember, Alice?" Her father countered in his gruff tone.

Hannah and David shared a knowing look in the front and their eyes gave off an almost silent dare of who would be the one to fill her father in on the turn of events between them.

David lost.

"'Bout that." Before he could continue, the vehicle behind them laid on their horn with so much vigor that David felt forced out of his parking spot and hit the gas to join the masses Driving away from the airport.

"'About that' what?" Her dad asked from the back seat in the same tone he'd used before.

David kept his eyes on the road when he reached over and entwined their fingers, then raised them up just in case her father couldn't see the action.

"Jim, don't you dare ruin this trip," her mom warned. "I don't want you spending this visit interrogating the poor boy."

"Boy?" Her dad shouted out. "You did see him, didn't you, Alice?"

"I did. And I have to admit, he is enjoyable to look at."

Hannah jerked her head toward her mother and glared, but when her eyes shifted to David, all he showed was that devilish grin.

"How old are you, Mr. Givens?"

"Call me David," he told her dad casually. "I'm thirty-seven."

"My daughter is twenty-five."

"I'm aware."

David seemed to take her dad's scolding in stride. He wasn't that intimidating of a man, however; not compared to David. They were about the same height, but her dad looked like an accountant, probably because he was, while David looked like a man who could take you down with a single finger.

"And that doesn't bother you?" Her dad asked.

David shook his head, then made a turn on a side street. "Nope. But something tells me it bothers you."

"Honey, we're his guests for the week. Could you just try not to rock the boat?" Her mom begged.

Her mom was the one who took life in stride and was the yin to his yang. She didn't let many things bother her and instead of taking life one day at a time, she seemed to take it one moment at a time. She didn't allow the past to bother her or the future to worry her. She accepted that any problem faced would usually feel insignificant later on, so didn't get hung up on the little things.

Her father, on the other hand, focused on every detail. He often focused on the worst in anything rather than the joy. Everything was a dollar sign either being gained or taken away. If you did something incorrectly, he didn't just tell you how to do it right, but told you just how wrong you were, adding all the big consequences to it.

If she didn't wash her car regularly during the winter, she wasn't being responsible with her investment and was lectured on the consequences of salt. If she didn't put a DVD back in the case, he would ask why she spent money on something that she was just going to scratch up and allow to collect dust.

He was also a very loving man. She and her mother both knew that. He did, however, always seem to have trouble expressing that. Because his mind was constantly working overtime and expecting the worst out of every situation, it was difficult for him to focus on all the good life had to offer.

Hannah hoped that one day in the future, her mom would rub off on him just a little, and he'd be able to enjoy life for what it was.

"Of course it bothers me that my daughter is dating a man twelve years older than her!" Her father shouted from the back seat.

David took the next turn and jumped onto the interstate, hitting the gas to meet up with the speed. "I'm financially responsible, own my own business, and enjoy living a quiet life, same as her. I don't drink heavily, don't do drugs and with years in the military, I can not just make her feel safe, but make sure she is safe. I make my own furniture, own my own house, I cook and I clean. I also care deeply for her and intend on showing that every damn day. So I can't help but wonder what your other requirements are."

Her mother laughed behind her. "Well, David, I think you're just adorable."

Adorable wouldn't normally be a word used to describe David, but he had been just that over the last few days. She'd let her mother use any word choice on him so long as it was positive, however. While her mother was an easy going woman, she wasn't so easy to impress when it came to the men she dated. If her mother had any kind words that didn't seem forced this early on, it was a vast victory.

Chapter Fifteen

"Well I have to say, David, this meal is just delicious," her mom told him from across the table before she wiped her mouth on the gray linen napkin. "I think you might be in the wrong business."

David smiled warmly at her mom. "I've been thinkin' the same thing."

"Owning a bar and owning a restaurant are two very different things," her dad chimed in, remaining ever the critic. "The startup costs can be astronomical. Add that to the building itself, insurance costs, employees... You'd be surprised on how fast it can add up. Unless you have a spare half million or more laying around, you'd need a bank loan-"

"Three," David said a bit randomly before taking a bite of his chicken wellington.

"Pardon?"

"I have a spare three million."

"Sweetheart," her mom began, placing her hand on Hannah's arm. "Are you dating a millionaire?"

All Hannah could think to do was shrug. Money was never a big deal for her. It was a nice thing to have and certainly made life easier to live, but she never looked down on people who didn't have much to spare and didn't put anyone on a pedestal who did have it. It was one of those things that had importance, but also wasn't that important when compared to other traits. "I guess so," she muttered before taking another bite of her dinner.

When she heard David's quiet chuckle, Hannah looked and saw him just shaking his head as he looked down at his plate.

"If you are a millionaire, David, I can't help but wonder why you own a bar on the wrong side of the tracks, so to speak."

While Hannah didn't care much about financial means, her dad did, which was why she wondered why her dad was still pushing him.

"Maybe be—cause that's the kind of g-guy he is," Hannah spoke.

Her dad jerked his fork into the air and pointed it at her from across the table. "A guy from the wrong side of the track."

He was unbelievable, and not in a good way. He may have been a great husband and father, but his judgement of others was his downfall.

Everyone had a story and none of them were any different. But while Hannah tried to look at every warm body and see a person with a past, present and future, her dad took things at face value. When he saw a homeless person, all he saw was a bum. He didn't think about what led them there or the hardships they were facing or their personal demons.

"A g-guy who does—n't let mon—ey def—ine him," Hannah corrected.

"Need I remind you, sweetheart," her mom intervened as she
stabbed a piece of broccoli with her fork and brought it toward her
mouth. "That we are guests in his house and if anyone spoke to you
this way in your house, you'd be kicking them out right about now."

David wiped his mouth with his napkin and dropped it on his
plate. "Would you rather I be a stockbroker who's puts his job before
everything else and has an apartment no one knows about where he
can take his affairs to?" He didn't wait for her dad's reply. "Yes, I own
a bar and yes, it's in a shitty ass neighborhood. But people aren't what
they do for a living."

"I realize that, Mr. Givens, but Hannah isn't cut out for that kind
of life. She doesn't belong working on the other side of the tracks.
That isn't who she is. She comes from a good family."

David pushed his plate to the side. "I'm not gonna lie, my clientele
can be a rough and rowdy group. There's fights I gotta break up and
folks I gotta keep in line. Have you ever been in a fight, Jim?"

"Of course not!" Her dad said with a swift shake of his head. "A
little rough housing in college, but that was all in good fun."

A forced smile appeared on David's face. "I've been in more than
my fair share, so if you insinuate that my family aren't good people
again, you'll find yourself in one and you'll lose."

Hannah hung her head, not wanting to look at either man at that
moment and only wished it was possible to teleport out of a room.

She'd rather be just about anywhere else in that moment than at that table.

"He didn't mean anything by it, David," her mother tried to defend, but they all knew the truth.

"I know your husband is just trying to test my limits, but he found them and that is not a line I recommend he cross. I'm a patient man and can handle a little interrogation, but I'll only be pushed so much before I start pushing back."

"I can't be—lieve you," Hannah shouted at her father as she paced her small kitchen.

It hadn't gotten much better after her dad backed down. Instead it got eerily quiet. Her mom attempted to strike up new conversation options to no avail. It was so much worse than any other time she'd introduced a guy to her parents, despite one of them seeming to be on board.

Her dad ran his hands through his silver hair as he stood in the center of her living room and her mom sat on the couch. "He is not the man for you, Hannah. I don't care how much money he has, the guy is a deviant. He threatened me with violence for Christ sake."

"And I'm sur—prised it took him th-that long! You've been on his c-case since you g-g-got here. You bas—ic—ally called him a sh-shit bag in his own house!"

"You watch your mouth, young lady," her dad scolded as he pointed a finger.

"No," she fired back. "Ev—er since the acc—id—ent, you have been treat—ing me like a child. But I'm not a child, dad, I'm a grown ass wo—man. I can swear and go out by my—self and have sex and have a re—la—tion—ship with who—ever the hell I want! I'm not fuck—ing fee—ble and I'm not brok—en. I can make dec—sions for myself!"

"Hannah," her mother spoke up, remaining strangely silent up until then. "Why don't you go stay with David tonight?"

Her dad shook his head. "Oh, no-"

Her mom remained slouched in the corner of the couch, rubbing at her right temple for the last five minutes. This was the first time she'd even looked up and she she did, it was to look at her husband. "We raised a strong woman, honey. You aren't going to get anywhere by telling our twenty-five year old daughter who she can and can't date. This isn't a 'your house, your rules' anymore, this is her house and her life and his property and unless you want to get your ass kicked off this property and spend Thanksgiving all by yourself, I suggest you close your mouth and open your eyes."

After a half a minute of complete silence, her mom lifted herself off the couch, looking exhausted by the long day or perhaps just exhausted by her husband. "Our daughter is happy. After living the last three years in misery, she's actually happy and I'm not going to let you try to sabotage that because the only thing you'll end up sabotaging is your relationship with her."

Hannah didn't trust herself to keep her cool in all this and it appeared as if her mom had a better chance of getting through to him than she did, so she grabbed her phone off the end table and walked out the front door, ignoring her dad's comments to stay put.

Her mom was right. She'd been living the last three years in misery. The first year was unbearable. It was if her soul and mind had been moved into another body she didn't recognize and could not control. Hannah was angry as hell for a long time. After that anger faded, she'd thought she'd become better at masking her emotions, though it was all so much worse when she was stuck with only the sadness of a life she could no longer live.

While all other's assumed she was fine, Hannah's mother saw the truth it seemed. She'd seen the anger as well as the sadness. And now, three years later, she was able to see the happiness that Hannah hadn't felt since before the accident.

David stood by the open front door as she passed through, seeming to have expected her return. "Didn't go quite like I planned."

Hannah shrugged as she walked into the house. "My mom likes you. My dad will t-too, once he gets his head out of his ass."

David let out a low chuckle, closed the door, and put his arms around her. "He's just being protective. I knew as soon as we picked 'em up from the airport that he wasn't gonna be an easy man to impress, and I can respect that.

"So," David continued, giving her body a light squeeze. "How 'bout we save the mess in the kitchen for the morning and you and I go to bed?"

Hannah placed a soft kiss on his lips, his scruffy face tickling her nose. "Bed sounds good."

Chapter Sixteen

There was no feeling quite like waking up in the arms of a strong, beautiful man. Every night since they began sharing a bed, David held her with such a gentle, loving touch, yet with a firm grasp as if he worried she would disappear in the night.

Hannah loved the smell of his shoulder length hair as it draped across the top of her head. She loved the feel of his heartbeat beneath the palm of her had she rested it atop his naked chest. Loved the sound of his gentle breaths interrupted by an occasional whimper.

This is what she'd been missing all of her life. Jerry Maguire was right after all. One person could truly complete another.

It wasn't until the night before when her father seemed determined that this relationship not happen that Hannah felt an overwhelming worry of losing all of this. Now, having David's arms holding her close, it became all she wanted. Her mom was right. This was her first time being content in forever.

David let out a groan and turned their bodies as one so they rested on their sides. It was then she felt something press against her ass and wished like hell they slept naked so she could feel his erection against her bare skin. His breaths remained the same as they were before, appearing to still be asleep, so Hannah risked a reach around between their bodies. As soon as she made contact, his morning wood came out of the hole of the boxers and slid into her hand.

Honestly, she hadn't meant for that to happen, but she also wasn't in the least bit sorry about it. When David's breathing hitched, Hannah knew she'd been caught.

"My dick is in your hand," he spoke in a tired sort of groan.

"Hmm-mmm."

"Why is it in your hand, Hannah?"

Hannah turned her head just a little enough to be closer to him but not so close to subject him to her morning breath. "Be—cause it want—ed to be."

David chuckled behind her. "I don't doubt it."

When it appeared he had no intention smacking her hand away or telling her 'not until your parents leave town', Hannah threw caution to the wind and explored his body, moving her hand from the center up to the head, noticing a slight curve as she reached the top, then back down again until she began stroking him firmly at a slow pace.

David's lips pressed against her neck and the arm that rested on her stomach travelled below the fabric of her shirt, sliding upward until it cupped her breast. A breathless sigh escaped his mouth and his fingers clenched her nipple while his hips thrust his erection in her grasp.

"I was planning on showing some restraint with you, ya know," she heard him say behind her.

"Show all the re—straint you want. Does—n't mean I have to."

But it didn't appear either of them had a choice when the sound of his front door bell sang out into the quiet air.

"Fuck me," he muttered, a bite in his tone. "I'm guessing that's your parents, and I ain't gunna answer the door with a hard-on."

It was a hysterical sight to imagine, but if there was any hope of her dad accepting David as her boyfriend, introducing him to his morning erection probably wasn't the best way to go about making that happen.

So Hannah let go of his erection, much to her dismay, and turned around in his grasp, placing a small closed-lipped kiss on his lips and another on his bare chest before forcing herself out of the bed and left David all alone sprawled out on the bed. She took in the glorious sight one last time then trotted out of the room, down the hall and over to the front door, seeing only her mother standing there before she opened it.

"Did I interrupt anything?" Her mom asked, a sly smile on her face.

Blunt was the best word to describe her mom. She said exactly what was on her mind and to hell with one anyone thought about it.

Hannah held up her hand and placed her pointer and thumb a quarter of an inch apart. "Lit—tle bit."

A light pink crept onto her mother's cheeks and she ran her fingers through her light brown curly hair. "I'd offer to come back, but I probably already killed the mood, didn't I?"

Before Hannah could respond, David came out in plaid pajama pants and a black t-shirt, his hair in disarray. "Morning."

"Ah," her mom hollered in a chipper tone. "I see I didn't entirely kill the mood."

Hannah followed her mother's stare to David and noticed his erection hadn't yet gone down completely.

Rather than reply, David just spun his heals and went right back down the hall. A moment later, a light tap came from behind them and Hannah jumped before turning around and noticing her father at the door.

Her mom went ahead and opened it. "How was the couch?" She asked with a devilish grin.

Her dad was already fully dressed. "Much more comfortable than it looked."

"Well, shucks. That's too bad. I was sort of hoping there'd be a broken spring in there or something."

So her mother had forced her dad to sleep on the couch as punishment for his behavior the night before, which was a nice change of pace and proof that he'd acted just as out of line as Hannah suspected.

"There's no coffee maker in that apartment," her father said gruffly, ignoring her mother's comment.

Hannah shook her head. "That's because I don't drink coffee. My medications don't mix well with a lot of caffeine."

She went into the kitchen and opened the fridge to get her juice just as David walked back out wearing dark blue jeans. Hannah took a closer look to confirm his erection had finally gone down, which it fortunately had.

"Good morning," he said, either to her mother once again or her father. He didn't look at either of them, but rather kept his eyes on Hannah until he reached her, putting his arm around her stomach and placing a soft kiss on her temple.

"I'll get some coffee started," he spoke after placing one more kiss on her cheek. "Does anyone want some breakfast?"

Her mother walked over, her hand placed on her stomach. "I'm still full from last night. Honestly, David, you really do have a gift. I don't know anyone who can cook like you."

Because her mother always spoke the truth, no matter how uncomfortable that truth may be, Hannah knew her mother's compliment was genuine. "I've gained at least t-three pounds since mov—ing here."

David leaned into her, placing his lips close to her ear. "And you're even sexier for it."

Hannah was a size six currently. She'd been many sizes prior to that and this was her preferred. But if this relationship stuck, she didn't doubt she'd shoot up to a ten by the end of the year.

David went back to making coffee while her dad approached the kitchen area, sitting on the stool on the other side of the kitchen island. "I wanted to apologize for my behavior last night, David," he began. "It was uncalled for. I'm afraid I was taken by surprise with the relationship and lashed out. Honestly, I always thought that Hannah and Shawn would get back together someday-"

"Certainly not for a lack of trying on the Bible salesman's part."

Her dad scrunched his face. "Huh?"

"Never mind," David said with a shake of his head and he filled the back of the coffee maker with water and pressed 'start'. "Listen, I get that you saw this big future for your daughter with the white picket fence and shit and I'm sorry that changed for her. Hannah got dealt a bad fucking hand and if I could take her pain away and make it my own, I'd do it without a second thought. But that ain't in my power.

"What is in my power is making sure she's taken care of and loved every single day. And I'm gonna do that with or without your permission or blessing."

Hannah was focused on that single word that caused a rush of electricity through her body. A word he said so casually despite likely rarely using it. And while it was clear both her parents had also heard him use that word, neither of them said anything and David poured her juice as if it were just another word in the dictionary.

Chapter Eighteen

That single word David spoke remained in Hannah's thoughts throughout the day. They'd known each other for close to three weeks at that point; not nearly enough time for real love to blossom from the seed of introduction. Love didn't come with one big wave, crashing down on you in a single moment, but rather from all the small moments collecting and building up.

David had gone from a life of one night stands after getting his heart broken many years ago. More likely, he was just in love with the idea of love, wanting to give his heart to someone again with the hopes of it being taken care of this time around. She could see herself falling in love with David Givens. He was uncharacteristically handsome, thoughtful, with a strong body and a mind to match.

More than anything, he cared for her in a way Hannah never expected to have again in this life. He took her under his wing and gave her shelter, but she didn't feel like a charity case. When he looked at her or listened when she spoke, she didn't feel less than. Around him, she was rid of the label of 'broken person' and was only Hannah; a young woman on her very own, terrifying adventure of possibilities and second chances.

So was there a possibility that he truly did love her?

Were they each other's second chance?

"You've been thinking about it all day," her mom noticed as they walked the streets of the small town nearest David's house.

No one had mentioned the end to the conversation he had with her father. Her dad went off to explore the larger city, David went to check on the bar and confirm it'd been cleaned up from that single terrible night, while her and her mother chose a more quiet day. Although no one had spoken about it, at least not to Hannah, it remained heavy in the air.

"How long d-did it take you to fall in l-love with dad?" Hannah asked her mother.

Her mom let out a snicker as she paused to admire a cashmere sweater dress in one of the shop windows. "Truth is, I found your father dull as can be for the first several dates, but your aunt Becky kept assuring me that it just takes awhile for him to open up. He did eventually, but it was a long time before I really started to fall for him."

Hannah knew her parents were introduced by her aunt, but that was the only part of the story she'd heard about how they ended up together. She supposed if it was an adorable story, she would have heard more. "Why did you start to fall for him?"

Her mom pried her eyes away from the pretty dress in the window and turned to Hannah, running her fingers through her short dark blond hair and licking her lips. "One day he came over to pick me up for a date and my elderly neighbor was just getting home from the grocery store. She was so tiny and fragile and it took her a good minute to walk even a few steps.

"He asked me about her, but I didn't know much. All I knew was that she'd never married, had no children and had lived with her twin sister after her husband died. Her twin had died about a year prior and I never really saw her have any company over.

"Anyhow, he trotted over to her and took the groceries out of her hands and helped her up her porch steps and into the house. When he didn't come out after a few minutes, I went over there and saw he was helping to put groceries away. He asked if it would be okay to have dinner in with his new friend. That night I realized he had this big old heart he'd kept hidden away. We moved in together a few months later into a bigger place, but he still insisted on going over there a couple of times a month to have dinner with her, all the way up until she died two years later.

"A year later, we got married and a year after that we had a beautiful baby girl he wanted to name after her, as a way to show that she was remembered. He told me that was a fear he'd had when he was single; that he would die alone and be forgotten. Your dad didn't want that for her."

Just as she didn't know much about how her parents ended up together, Hannah also knew very little about how she was named. 'You were named after a lovely woman we knew years ago,' was all she was told.

Normally Hannah would want to know every bit about that woman there was to know, especially since she'd unintentionally played Cupid for her parents. Her mind was on a different path, however, unwilling to deviate.

It had taken Hannah several months before she began to fall in love with Shawn. Was it possible for real love to form in a fraction of that time?

Before Hannah could ask that question aloud, she saw David walking down the street toward them, a smile on his face like none other she'd seen before. Once he reached her, David grabbed her hand and pulled her in the direction he'd just come from. "Come on, I wanna show you somethin'."

Hannah through a quick glance toward her mother, who only shrugged, and followed David's quick pace as fast as she could, her mom not far behind. They'd gone about a block and a half when David stopped abruptly, taking her by the shoulders and moving her body away from the street.

"What do ya think?"

Hannah looked around her without the slightest clue what she was meant to be looking at. Then her eyes caught a 'for sale' sign in the window of the building she was facing. She took two steps forward, close enough to peer through the window. Though it was more or less empty inside, the large space and bar near the back confirmed it was a restaurant. "You're ser—iou—sly think—ing a-b-b-out this, are—n't you?"

David had shared his dream of owning a restaurant briefly, but she remembered how his eyes lit up when he spoke of it. Still, she hadn't realized just how soon he wanted that dream to become a reality.

"Realtor gave me a key," he said, shoving the piece of metal into the lock and turning it before he pushed open the door just as her mom caught up.

Despite it being only mid-afternoon, it was fairly dark inside the building and David flipped the light switches beside them to bring the building to life. Hannah tried her best to imagine the space in all it's glory. The walls would be better suited a different color than the dark red they currently were; something quite a bit lighter to make it feel less drab.

"I'm not sure what I would do with this area," David began, pointing at a smaller section in front of the bar. "It's only big enough for about four tables. Maybe just have it as a waiting area."

"You could serve drink and appetizers there," her mom suggested. "Have a nice tapas menu. You could fit a good six bistro tables there and put a couple of couches over there with a coffee table for larger parties that are waiting or just looking for a quick bite."

"You're ser—i—ous?" Hannah asked once again.

David crossed his arms and she watched as his grin grew to nearly half the size of his face. "Oh, I'm serious. I'm gunna need your help when it comes to decorating and tables and all that shit."

By the look of his house, as well as the furnished apartment she was living in, David didn't need any help in that department. His taste was worlds better than her own, but he wanted to include her and Hannah would try her best not to steer him wrong.

"Tell me you like it. Please. I'm dying here, darlin'."

Hannah looked around once more. Restaurant owning was a risky business and an exhausting one. But David was a hard worker and didn't seem to shy away from a risk. More than anything, she was just happy that he was making his own dreams come true. "I love it," she responded finally.

In an instant, David's arms were wrapped around her and he was spinning her body around with the greatest of ease.

Chapter Nineteen

"I 've never seen him like this."

Hannah followed Meggie's gaze to where it lay on David as he was standing by the kitchen island going through paperwork with her dad. It was strange seeing both men so focused with the bickering having gone away, only leaving a mutual determination in its stead.

"He's ex—cit—ed," she agreed after a few quiet moments, a smile playing on her lips as she admired the two men in her life working side by side.

An airy laugh escaped Meggie as she sat down on the wooden chair beside her, the cool autumn breeze whisking their hair every which way. "It's not just that. I've seen that man excited a hundred times, Hannah, but I've never seen him happy. Not really."

It was thanksgiving, and as soon as the men had eaten, they were back to work on their master plan. They were crunching numbers, organizing different aspects of the business into files, and, unless Hannah's eyes were playing tricks on her, she'd even seen her father pat him on the back.

The women sat in the living room, complaining of full stomachs glancing at the pie selection, while drinking wine and admiring the men's hard work.

"I'm sure you've seen him hap—py," Hannah argued, before taking a drink of her sparkling juice, assuming that there must have been a handful of times Meggie had seen David happy and excited.

Meggie leaned back on the suede couch and shook her head. "Nope. He has two looks; 'I don't give a shit' and a scowl. Even when things are going great for him, that man finds one negative thing and harps on it. You make him happy, Hannah. You make him happy and hopeful and all that other sappy shit."

Her mom bumped Meggie with her elbow. "He said the 'L' word yesterday. Didn't even look like it phased him."

"What the flying monkey's is going on with him," Meggie asked, trying to clear up her language a little. "Did you say it back?"

"He said it in front of my par—ents, like it was the most nat—ur—al thing in the world to say. But since he was—n't say—ing it to me, so much as my dad, I don't think he ex—expect—ed me to res—pond."

"What would you have said?" Meggie asked, looking utterly amazed at the change of conversation.

Hannah shrugged. "'Thank you'?" What a terrible decision that would have made, but it wasn't as if she could say it back. They'd only kissed a few times and hadn't been intimate. They hadn't even gone on a single date yet. "I love him as a person and as a friend, but it takes a little longer for me to feel that kind of love."

"Are you sure that wasn't how he meant it? Loving you as a person and a friend?"

The way he said it caused Hannah to really think about it, playing the entire conversation again in her mind, hoping to get every detail just as it was.

'What is in my power is making sure she's taken care of and loved every single day.' The statement was innocent enough on it's own... probably. Her parents had taken care of her and loved her every single day. But followed by, 'I'm gonna do that with or without your permission or blessing," caused Hannah to wonder why he'd need or bother with anyone's opinion when it came to something so innocent.

She'd intended on asking her mom for her opinion on all of it earlier that day, but David had shown up and the conversation came to an abrupt end.

Unable to take it anymore, Hannah set her glass down, rose from the couch, and forced her sluggish, food-filled body over to the kitchen area, grabbed David's arm, and tugged until he relented to follow. With him living in a mostly glass house, there were few places inside or outside to talk without eyes watching them. Even the bedrooms all had windows in the hallway, none of the curtains drawn right now, to see the windows in the hallways overlooking the pool.

Although she could have drawn the curtain, Hannah wasn't certain a bedroom was the right location to have a conversation like this, so she grabbed his hand and let him out to the pool, sitting with her back turned to the main portion of the house while David closed the door behind him.

"What he hell's goin' on, Hannah?"

"Love," she answered quick so as not to chicken out. "You said y-you loved m-me yes—ter—day."

David ran his fingers though his longer hair, his narrowed eyes suddenly filling with a slight sparkle. "That's what's making you all batshit crazy?"

Hannah didn't realize she had been acting any amount of 'batshit crazy', but her emotions and confusion over his own may have gotten the best of her over the last thirty plus hours.

He walked over to her with casual stride, knelt down, and covered her hands with his own. "There's a lot a ways to love someone, Hannah, and I love you in a lot of important ways, just not the way you're thinkin'. Given time, I don't doubt I will, but I just ain't there yet. If you do, that's okay. I won't freak out or nothin'. But in my eyes, you gotta get to know all the good and all the bad in someone before you can really love 'em, and we're just startin' to get to know each other."

Hannah let out a slow, long breath. "I w-w-was th-think—ing the s-same. I was s-scared that you were there, and I was—n't."

"I ain't there yet, darlin', but I'll let you know when I am. Deal?"

She nodded, relief filling her once she new she had the sort of love from David she was ready to accept.

Chapter Twenty

Although they were celebrating Christmas a full month early with no snow on the ground, Hannah felt blissfully normal for the first time in years.

Her parents were smiling, appearing stress-free and seeming to finally enjoy being around each other for the first time on this vacation after her fathers rough start. Meggie was also smiling, wearing a lavender angora sweater with most of her piercings taken out and her tattoos covered, resembling the girl she went to high school with all those years ago.

And there Hannah was, her boyfriend's arm around her on the couch, rubbing small circles against her shirt with his thumb, seeming finally relaxed after the terrible turn of events the week before.

She hadn't told her parents about that night. They didn't know about the robbery, or about David taking one man's life while another was still hospitalized and the third was in jail. They weren't aware of him randomly leaving the house during their stay was because police needed to talk to him about what occurred. Now that David had gained a strong measure of acceptance by her parents, Hannah wasn't about to risk it being tainted.

With all the presents unwrapped, David pushed himself off the couch and grabbed a garbage bag from the kitchen, collecting all the small and large pieces of wrapping paper spread throughout the living room.

Hannah's mother left her dad's side and walked over to plop on the couch beside her. "That man of yours is damn good looking, kiddo. I could watch him bend over all day."

Through the living room was fairly large, David was well within hearing distance and let out a soft laugh.

Though Hannah's skin flushed with embarrassment, she took it as a compliment if only for the simple fact that although there was a rocky start with her dad, they'd warmed up to David in record time.

Hearing 'that man of yours' still threw her. A few weeks ago, Hannah thought she'd made the biggest mistake of her life when she pulled up across the street from the bar. Everything about it made her want to pull a u-turn and high-tail it back to where she came from.

Then David picked her up and she looked into his pale blue eyes and all the world grew still for a single moment in the vastness of time. In his arms she felt safety. In his eyes she found kindness. In his heartbeat she found calm. In his face she found beauty amongst the scars.

It was those scars that told her David's past had a darkness. If she'd met him only a few years ago, maybe that darkness would have been difficult to accept. Maybe it would have been something to fear. But now, Hannah found a comfort in it. David wasn't some epitome of perfection. She didn't feel as if she weighing him down with her baggage and endless complications. There were no feelings of holding him back now.

All that wrapped together was truly remarkable.

When her mother spoke again, it was in a much quieter voice. "I don't know what that boy's past is, Hannah, and I'm not sure I want to know. All I need to know is that he's looking at the future right now and that future includes you. I knew a few guys like him in my time, and that's a pretty big thing, letting someone be a part of your life like that."

She had no idea. Or maybe she did. Either way, Meggie had told Hannah what kind of guy he was before she moved here, and David more or less confirmed it. So it really was a big thing for him to see her in his future when he hadn't looked passed the next morning before she came along.

As soon as Hannah woke up in that hospital bed three and a half years earlier and saw Shawn asleep in the chair beside her, she still loved him. Hannah had no idea at the time to what measure her life changed, but as the seconds turned to minutes, the minutes to hours, and the hours to days, Shawn was slipping away from her future like pages being unwritten.

Now that Hannah looked back, she saw her life story taking another turn and leading her to David in this surreal and somewhat morbid way she wouldn't change for anything.

It was unnerving that the worst thing ever to happen in her life brought her to this place and this person.

Then it happened. Hannah's heart opened up and showed her what she was feeling was indeed love. It was strange considering she thought for sure love happened in stages. But there it was. Hannah thought about him constantly and had a smile on her face when she saw him. She found herself randomly staring at him and allowing this calmness and happiness to sink into her. The fact that he was becoming a happier person since being with her filled her with pride and joy. He was giving her the strength to try new things from staying in an overwhelming city to working at a busy bar to more or less moving in with a stranger.

Hannah ran her fingers through her auburn hair and took a deep breath. She hadn't come to this town to fall in love, but it was exactly what happened.

It was true she didn't yet know every detail about David. Much of it was remained hidden away or were things he hadn't yet shared. But what she did know about him, good and bad, were loved. If last weeks shooting hadn't scared her, Hannah doubted that anything could.

She stood and walked out by the pool, feeling her mothers eyes on her as she closed the door and sat down out there. The chlorine filled her lungs, while the warmth from the water dampened her skin with its humidity. It was always one of her favorite smells. Ever since she was young, she loved to swim. These days it felt more like a chore to keep her body working properly, but was forever an escape for her.

When the door opened and closed behind her, Hannah turned to see David approach.

"I love you." The words just sort of tumbled out of her mouth, but Hannah meant all three of them. Love wasn't meant to happen so quickly, but there it was and every ounce of it felt so genuine that it didn't need to be denied or suppressed.

David paused for a moment, then began to walk again and sat down beside her with one side of his mouth curved up into that mischievous smile. "You do, huh?"

Hannah nodded her confirmation. Since he'd told her yesterday that it was completely okay with him if she did feel it, Hannah didn't want to omit the truth. She didn't want to keep it inside. Being around David these last few weeks, she'd been taking risks and each one felt more liberating than the last.

"I know it's fast, and I know we don't know each oth—er that well, but all the signs are there, and I can't just ig—nore them."

David scratched at the stubble on his face, then moved his hand up to his shoulder length hair before propping his elbows against the table in front of them. "You're right, darlin', we don't know each other that well. You don't know about all the shit I did for the military, and I ain't ready to tell you yet because I'm scared as hell of seeing you walk out that door and never lookin' back.

"My gut tells me you'll stick around, but my head's still getting in the way of that. When I get up the courage, I'll tell you. If you wanna give me your heart after that, I'd be more than happy to take it and take damn good care of it.

"You're it for me, Hannah. These weeks we've spent together, they've been the best of my life and taken me to a place I never thought I'd find. But I can't let myself fall in love with you until you know everything, and still love me back."

Hannah nodded her understanding. The beautifully scarred man beside her had a fear that she couldn't handle the truth, just as she constantly had a fear of everyone's pity. "When you're read—dy, you tell me. I'll still be here."

Chapter Twenty-One

"Hannah?" David spoke when she remained quiet.

He did open up. Once he finally gained the courage, he told her something every day. He started small and at the beginning, telling her about his childhood and family. As his stories grew with his age, Hannah began to mentally prepare herself for the truth he'd kept hidden.

This story was different from the others. It wasn't just his first kill for the military, but that of a child soldier. David said he couldn't have been older than twelve, and hadn't taken the shot until the gun pointed at his friend.

Hannah gave him a squeeze and draped her bare leg across his own beneath the sheets, then placed her hand on his naked chest.

She saw it coming; not the details, but that this was the story he worried about telling her. She could feel the despair and hesitance heavy in the air. He'd also taken his time making love to her. Normally he was passionate, but this time he'd been so gentle and slow, much like their first time together.

Everything about it felt different, like he was committing every touch to memory in case she walked out the door.

"I still love you," she whispered against his chest hair. So far she'd said that after every story.

It wasn't easy waiting for and was even more difficult hearing, but David was right. In order to give your entire heart to someone, who have to know and accept all of the worst. And she did. Despite all of his painful truths, Hannah loved him.

A quiet sigh escaped the lips above her and he squeezed her naked body tight against his own. "You sure?"

"Does it get much worse than that?" Hannah asked, hoping he understood the question.

His stories had only recently reached his twenties. He'd joined the military when he turned eighteen, and David told her he'd only retired, or whatever the military called it, five years ago. That meant there were many more stories to come.

"That was the worst thing I ever had to do. It wasn't the worst thing I'd ever seen, though."

"Then yes, I'm sure I still love you. If you'd smoth—ered a b-ba—by or some—thing, I think I'd prob—ab—ly reach my li—mit, but you were pro—tect—ing a friend, and I get in that sit—u—a—tion you only have a s-sec—ond or two to make a dec—c-is—ion."

"Why do you love me?" David asked above her.

This wasn't a question that men normally asked. Granted, she'd only ever said 'I love you' to Shawn before she met David, but it still threw her to have David ask. So she took her time and thought. While she may have had many reasons, it would take her forever to list them all.

Then she thought back to when her parents were visiting and she remembered how it felt after her accident. Her once bright future just quietly vanished right in front of her eyes.

"When I woke up after the shoo—ting, ev—ery—thing a-b-bout my life was different. I did—n't feel like a had a place in my own life, or a fu—ture. All I had was a past that I could n-n-ev—er get back. Then you b-brushed the hair from my face, picked me up off the ground and let me into your life. Y-you found me a place in my life a—gain and showed me I had a fu—ture."

David let out a groan, slipped his hand out from beneath Hannah's neck, then laid his body to the side to look her in the eyes. "You're future's with me, darlin'. If you still want me, everything I got and everything I am is yours. That's a promise."

"That's a big prom—ise," Hannah replied, though she didn't doubt he'd keep it. She saw how much he felt for her and what he'd do for her.

That devilish smile took over David's face. "I'll promise you the world if you marry me."

Hannah's eyebrows furrowed and nose scrunched, wondering if she even heard him correctly. Of course, her hearing was one of the few things that remained intact. "You have—n't e—ven t-told m-m-me you loved me y-yet, and y-you're ask—ing me to mar—ry you?"

"'I love you' is a big step," David replied, his tone a teasing one. "You can't rush me into that shit."

Hannah balled her hand into a fist and whacked him in the chest with it. "But marr—iage is—n't a big step at all!"

David grabbed her hand, loosened the fist, and placed her hand atop his heart. "This thing right here has belonged to you the moment you stepped into my life, darlin'. I'm in love with the way you look at me like I ain't a broken piece of shit. I'm in love with the way you talk, and the way you feel against me. There's nothing about you I ain't in love with. I just had to make sure you loved all of me."

So when David told her a month ago he wasn't there yet, he was completely bullshitting. He was there, but knew that in order for her end to be real and trusted, Hannah would have to learn of all the dark truths he'd kept hidden away.

"I do," Hannah said. Not all of it was easy to hear, and she still hadn't heard it all. But if told her the worst of himself, and if he accepted the worst in her, things he seemed to find more endearing than anything, then she was all in. Forever.

"So... that's a yes?"

Just because Hannah was all in didn't mean she was ready for that. "Fuck you. You just told me you loved me ten sec—onds ago."

David gathered her up in his arms and his devilish smile turned into one of warmth. "Then move in with me."

That was also a big step, but she was already more or less living there now. Her things were still in the apartment above the garage, but Hannah hadn't spent a night away from him since her parents left town.

"Yes, I'll move in with you."

Cheers erupted from the television screen that was placed on low volume, and David lowered his lips to hers. "Happy New Year, dar-lin'," he spoke before placing a soft kiss against her lips.

As Hannah kissed him back with conviction, she already looked forward to the new year, something she hadn't felt for a very long time.

Epilogue

David watched as she moved to every single table of the restaurant in slow, calculated movements, making sure every place setting was perfectly straight and rearranging the flowers in the center for the fourth time. She'd wanted to help with so much more than that, but knew her limitations. Despite giving her a list of other tasks she could do that day, Hannah declined after scanning them, saying she didn't want to make a mess of opening night.

That was the best part about her. After years in the military and keeping his life in perfect order, she brought a chaos he never wanted to live without. When she'd made that giant mess of the dish room at the bar, her t-shirt and hair clinging to her skin, he'd just about lost it that moment; not because she'd created her own personal hurricane in the room, but because she was turning his life upside down and sideways.

David never realized how much he needed that until she walked into his life.

"You got yourself an interesting girl, David," his father said as he stood by his side, then rubbed at his gray beard. "Didn't get it at first.

When you told me you fell in love with someone with a brain injury, I thought she was gonna be retarded or somethin'."

David shot his father a glare, who quickly corrected himself. "I get that word ain't PC around here, but where we come from, where you come from, that ain't a big deal, so you don't gotta go makin' it one." His dad shook his head, then looked over at Hannah. "What I'm tryin' to say here is that girl is special, and not in the short bus kinda way. And she loves the hell out of your grumpy ass, which is a miracle all on its own."

Looking over at her, David leaned against the counter and took her all in, trying to focus on his father's final words rather than his redneck ramblings. He knew there was a hell of a lot more he needed to do in the final two hours of opening, but whenever he found himself looking at her, it somehow turned into this longterm commitment.

He took in every single movement she made as if it were the most awkward and beautiful dance in the world. She looked beautiful in her black, understated dress and wasn't yet showing. "She's pregnant," he told his father. "Still hasn't told me about it."

His father turned to him wide-eyed. "Then how the hell do you know?"

David shrugged before crossing his arms. "Found the little cap that goes on one of those home pregnancy tests on the bathroom floor. I remembered what they looked like when Jackie had me grab her some in high school."

"You had a pregnancy scare in high school and you never told me? Boy, what the hell is the matter with you?"

He turned to see his father's red face and couldn't help but to chuckle at it. "That was twenty years ago, pops. Anyhow, I dug through the trash until I found it and saw it was positive."

His dad turned to look at Hannah once again. "You gonna do the right thing by that girl? It's a sin, having a child out of wedlock."

It was his first tour in Iraq when David lost God. If he did exist, he figured the guy wasn't worth looking up to. Shit you see on the battlefield haunt you for the rest of your life. It was the easiest place in the world to lose your faith in God.

But this wasn't about him and God. This was about him and Hannah. "If I propose to her now, she'll feel like I'm just doin' it because she's pregnant. I fully plan to marry that woman and spend the rest of my life with her, but she's gotta know it's for her, not out of obligation."

His dad let out a heavy sigh, then sat on the bar stool behind him. "You okay with her being pregnant?"

The first few minutes, he'd just stared at the test and silently wigged out. They'd only been living together for five months and known each other for seven. But once he hid the test away back where it was found and she walked through the door trying to juggle the groceries she'd just bought, any and all fear disappeared.

That woman was the one he'd already planned to spend the rest of his life with. She'd breathed life into this house and into his world.

Hannah had broken down every single one of his walls without even trying, and he loved her for that.

Raising a child scared the crap out of him. Raising a child with her filled something in him he couldn't describe or comprehend.

David guessed she was dealing with her own fears. Hannah had been distracted this last week, and it wasn't because of the business. He didn't blame her. She'd never be able to teach the child how to read or write, help them with their homework, or so many other things a parent is meant to do. But she could give that child love. It was something she seemed never short on, and that was the most important thing.

"More than okay," David finally answered just before Hannah walked over, a subtle sway in her hips.

His dad gave him a nod and walked away, and David took Hannah in his arms. "If your dad hadn't taken over my office to go through all my bills, I'd be having my way with you right now. You know that, don't you?"

Hannah's cheeks blushed. It got him every damn time. "You're hap—py, right?" She asked once the blush faded. "I mean, this has been your dream for a long time, has—n't it?"

It was his dream, but not the dream. Once she'd walked into his life, he began dreaming in a way he'd never dared before. "I'm happy, darlin'. As long as I got you by my side, I'm happy. If this all blows up in my face, can't say I didn't try."

Hannah's gaze fell to the floor. "Lis—ten, there's some—thing I need t-to t-talk to you about t-to—mor—row. I know you're going to be busy-"

"I ain't never gonna be too busy for you," David told her as he lifted up her chin to look her in the eyes. "I'm always going to make time for you. For us."

It wasn't ideal, having a kid just as he was starting a business, but he'd make do. At least this time he was smart enough to hire a manager right off the bat. Two, actually. One for the kitchen and one for the floor. He wanted to make damn sure that he had time for the woman who changed his life.

She may have been the one who wanted to tell him, or maybe she didn't. Either way, David placed his hand between them and rested his palm against her small stomach. "We can do this, darlin'. We can have it all."

Her puzzled expression turned into a soft smile that kissed his lips over and over again.

The guy who lived his life at a dive bar and never saw the same girl twice now had a home, the love of his life by his side, and was going to start a family.

Life was some crazy shit, but he supposed that was the point. As soon as Hannah walked into his life, a hot mess laying on the dirty pavement, she became the family he never realized he needed. She became his home.

Lightning Source UK Ltd.
Milton Keynes UK
UKHW010645030123
414755UK00014B/484